ROSEMARY WELLS

TIMOTHY GOES TO SCHOOL

PUFFIN BOOKS

PUFFIN BOOKS
Published by the Penguin Group
Penguin Putnam Books for Young Readers, 345 Hudson Street, New York, New York 10014, U.S.A.
Penguin Books Ltd, 27 Wrights Lane, London W8 5TZ, England
Penguin Books Australia Ltd, Ringwood, Victoria, Australia
Penguin Books Canada Ltd, 10 Alcorn Avenue, Toronto, Ontario, Canada M4V 3B2
Penguin Books (N.Z.) Ltd, 182-190 Wairau Road, Auckland 10, New Zealand

Penguin Books Ltd, Registered Offices: Harmondsworth, Middlesex, England

First published in the United States of America by Dial Books for Young Readers,
a division of Penguin Books USA Inc., 1981

This edition with new illustrations published by Viking,
a division of Penguin Putnam Books for Young Readers, 2000

Published by Puffin Books, a division of Penguin Putnam Books for Young Readers, 2000

10 9

THE LIBRARY OF CONGRESS HAS CATALOGED THE DIAL EDITION AS FOLLOWS:
Wells, Rosemary / Timothy goes to school.
Summary: Timothy learns about being accepted and making friends
during the first week of his first year at school.
[1. School stories.] I. Title.
PZ7.W46843Ti [E] 80-20785
ISBN 0-8037-8948-3 / ISBN 0-8037-8949-1 (lib. bdg.)

Puffin Books ISBN 0-14-056742-9

Manufactured in China

The art for this book was prepared in the usual way: with watercolor,
pen and ink, gouache, pastel, and rubber stamps.

For Mimi Kayden

TIMOTHY'S mother made him a brand-new sunsuit for the first day of school.
"Hooray!" said Timothy.

Timothy went to school in his new sunsuit
with his new book and his new pencil.

"Good morning!" said Timothy.
"Good morning!" said Mrs. Jenkins.

"Timothy," said Mrs. Jenkins, "this is Claude. Claude, this is Timothy. I'm sure you'll be the best of friends."

A B C D E F G H

"Hello!" said Timothy.

"Nobody wears a sunsuit on the first day of school," said Claude.

During playtime Timothy hoped and
hoped that Claude would fall into a puddle.

But he didn't.

When Timothy came home, his mother asked,
"How was school today?"

"Nobody wears a sunsuit on the first day of
school," said Timothy.

"I will make you a beautiful new jacket,"
said Timothy's mother.

Timothy wore his new jacket the next day.

"Hello!" said Timothy to Claude.
"You're not supposed to wear party clothes
on the second day of school," said Claude.

All day Timothy wanted and wanted Claude
to make a mistake.

But he didn't.

When Timothy went home, his mother asked,
"How did it go?"

"You're not supposed to wear party clothes
on the second day of school," said Timothy.
"Don't worry," said Timothy's mother.
"Tomorrow you just wear something in-between
like everyone else."

The next day Timothy went to school in his favorite shirt.

"Look!" said Timothy. "You are wearing the same shirt I am!"

"No," said Claude, "*you* are wearing the same shirt that *I* am."

During lunch Timothy wished and wished
that Claude would have to eat all alone.

But he didn't.

After school Timothy's mother could not find
Timothy. "Where are you?" she called.
"I'm never going back to school," said Timothy.
"Why not?" called his mother.

"Because Claude is the smartest and the best at everything and he has all the friends," said Timothy.

"You'll feel better in your new football shirt," said Timothy's mother.

Timothy did not feel better in his new football shirt.

That morning Claude played the saxophone.
"I can't stand it anymore," said a voice next to
Timothy.

It was Violet.

"You can't stand what?" Timothy asked Violet.

"Grace!" said Violet. "She sings. She dances. She counts up to a thousand and she sits next to me!"

During playtime Timothy and Violet
stayed together.

Violet said, "I can't believe you've been here all along!"

"Will you come home and have cookies with me after school?" Timothy asked.

On the way home Timothy and Violet laughed
so much about Claude and Grace that they both
got the hiccups.

microwaving meats

microwave cooking library™

by barbara methven

If you aren't using your microwave oven to cook meat, you're missing many of the benefits of this important appliance. A microwave does more than defrost and cook meat quickly or reheat leftovers so they taste freshly cooked. Microwaving brings out the full flavor of good meat and keeps it moist and juicy. The one thing a microwave oven can't do is improve the quality of poor meat. Successful microwaving begins in the market. The informed shopper is a better cook.

Most people don't shop every day. Proper storage of meat in either the refrigerator or freezer is as important as careful buying.

There is no mystery in meat microwaving. Much of what you already know about conventional meat cookery applies to microwaving, too. Power levels serve the same purpose as oven and surface burner temperatures. Less tender cuts require different cooking techniques from naturally tender ones.

This book tells you what you need to know about meat and microwaving in step-by-step pictures. Learn what the microwave oven can do for the most important item on your menu.

Barbara Methven

Barbara Methven

CREDITS:
Design & Production: Cy DeCosse Creative Department, Inc.
Consultants: Joanne Crocker, Robert V. Decareau, Ph. D., Ron Drahos
Home Economists: Jill Crum, Carol Grones, Muriel Markel, Maria Rolandelli
Photographers: Michael Jensen, Ken Greer
Production Coordinators: Bernice Maehren, Michael Lundeby, Dan Marchetti, Nancy McDonough
Typesetting: Ellen Sorenson
Color Separations: Weston Engraving Co., Inc.
Printing: R. R. Donnelley & Sons Company

Additional volumes in the Microwave Cooking Library series are available from the publisher:

• Basic Microwaving
• Recipe Conversion for Microwave
• Microwave Baking & Desserts
• Microwaving Meals in 30 Minutes
• Microwaving on a Diet
• Microwaving Fruits & Vegetables
• Microwaving Convenience Foods
• Microwaving for Holidays & Parties
• Microwave Cooking for One & Two
• The Microwave & Freezer
• 101 Microwaving Secrets
• Microwaving Light & Healthy

Contents

What You Should Know About Microwaving Meat

Most people plan their menus and their food budget around meat. Preparing meat is the cook's most important task, and one of the benefits of a microwave oven.

Microwaved meat not only cooks faster, but generally shrinks less and retains more juices than conventionally cooked. Microwaving brings out the full flavor of fresh, quality meat.

Buy & Store Meat Wisely

Unfortunately, microwaving cannot improve meat which has been stored improperly or too long. Although it may not be spoiled, old meat contains volatile oils which vaporize during cooking. Since there is no heat in the oven to burn off vapors, their odor can be detected during microwaving. It disappears when the meat is done, and flavor is not affected.

Care Pays Off

The recipes and procedures in this book have been tested in all major brands of microwave ovens. They call for the minimum of attention (turning over, rotating or rearranging) needed for good results. If your oven is very fast or has an uneven cooking pattern, you may want to give the meat extra attention. If you have the time, this is a good idea even if your oven cooks evenly.

Shielding with foil is recommended for cuts which may overcook in some areas. You may also use shielding to minimize attention or protect spots which are browning too fast.

While microwaving often reduces shrinkage and moisture loss, shielding can cut losses even more, especially on large, rolled roasts. As the ends of roasts cook, they firm up and contract, causing the roast to bulge in the middle. Meat fibers separate so juices escape. When the ends are shielded for part of the cooking time, the middle firms up first, and the roast cooks evenly throughout.

Tastes Differ

There are regional differences in the types and quality of meat available, and even greater variations in personal preferences. Where several methods of microwaving are suggested, be guided by your own taste and conventional cooking experience. For some people, a sirloin tip roast is a dry roast, for others, it's a pot roast.

The cooks who developed this book differ like anyone else. One of them always covers a ham with plastic wrap and shields the top cut edge. Another covers only the cut surface of the ham, uses no shielding, and checks the meat more frequently.

Most of the taste-testers found no significant difference between less tender cuts microwaved at 50% (Medium) and 30% (Low). A few reported they would prefer to cook these cuts longer and have them more tender. Microwaving times are included for both power levels.

Test for Doneness & Standing Times

All the directions in this book include one or more tests for doneness. Many also require standing time. In some cases, meat which appears done needs time to tenderize or improve flavor. Roasts should be removed from the oven before they reach their finished internal temperature; they continue to cook while standing. This is important if you are fussy about the doneness of roast beef, or are microwaving a meat which should be served well done. Meat cooked to higher temperatures loses its ability to retain moisture; standing time cooks it through without drying it out.

Meat Characteristics & Microwaving

Several meat characteristics affect the way foods cook. The amount and distribution of fat are most important. Other factors are the amount and position of bone, shape and size of meat. Finally, tenderness of meat determines the cooking method used.

Well marbled meat is more tender than very lean meat. The thin veins of interior fat give meat a fine grain, add flavor and help retain juices.

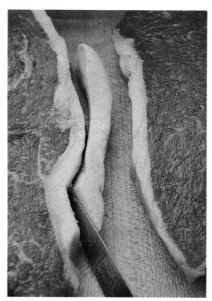

Even layers of fat on the outside of meat helps it microwave evenly. If the fat cover is heavier in one area, the meat next to it will cook faster and may overcook.

Drippings attract microwave energy away from the meat. When microwaving a roast, remove the drippings at intervals to speed cooking and prevent spatters.

Bone located within 1-in. of the surface reflects microwave energy into the meat around it, so these areas cook faster.

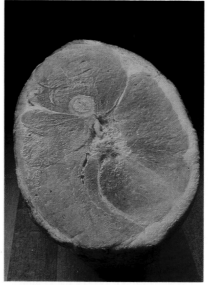

Center bones surrounded by more than 1-in. of meat have little effect on cooking.

Boneless meat cooks less rapidly but more evenly than bony meat.

Evenly shaped roasts, such as rolled rib or rump and boneless chuck cook evenly.

Irregular shapes cook faster in thin areas. Shield thin ends of roasts or bony tips of turkey legs with foil.

Arrange small irregular pieces, such as chops or drumsticks with thin parts to the center of dish.

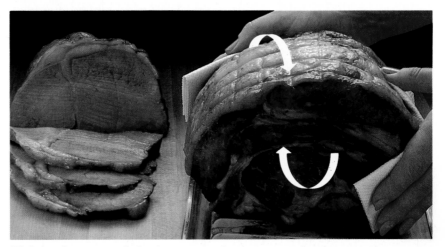

Small or thin pieces cook faster than large, thick ones. When meat is under 2 inches thick, microwave energy penetrates from all sides.

Thick pieces cook in the center by heat conduction, as they would conventionally. A large roast may cook more evenly if you turn it over twice: side to side as well as top to bottom.

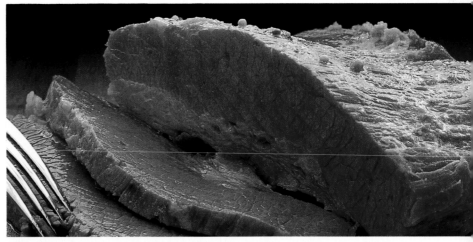

Less tender cuts and grades of meat need steam to tenderize. Cover them tightly.

Slower cooking also helps tenderize meat. If your oven has a 30% (Low) setting, you may lower the power level from 50% (Medium) and add ¼ to ⅓ more time.

Browning Meat

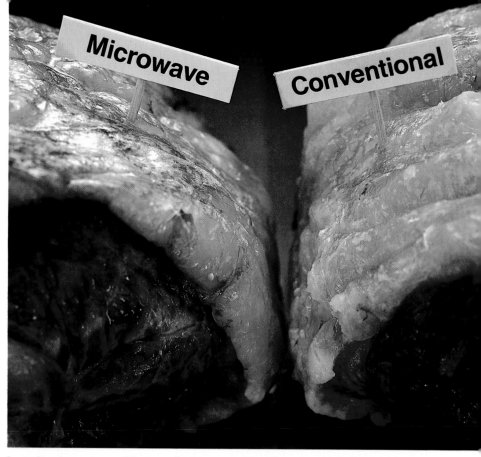

In both conventional and microwave cooking, browning of meat occurs when fat rises to the surface and gets hot enough to carbonize or become "partially burnt". In conventional cooking this happens automatically unless the meat is steamed or cooked in liquid. Surface moisture evaporates and the outside of the meat becomes dry and hard.

People who are accustomed to browning naturally feel that it adds an attractive appearance and appetite appeal, although they differ on the amount of browning needed. "Microwave families", especially the younger generation, are often indifferent to browning; they are satisfied when the meat looks cooked.

Many browning agents add flavor as well as color to meat. You may wish to make your own combinations.

In microwave cooking, a fatty meat which is cooked longer than 10 minutes will develop browning. Large pieces, like beef rib, leg of lamb or turkey breast will appear similar to conventionally cooked although the surface will not become dry.

Browning Agent Chart

Agent	Foods	Comments
Soy or Teriyaki Sauce	Hamburgers, Beef, Lamb, Pork, Poultry	Brush on meat; rub into poultry
Barbecue Sauce	Hamburgers, Beef, Lamb, Pork, Poultry	Brush on or pour over
Melted Butter and Paprika	Poultry	Brush on butter; sprinkle with paprika
Brown Bouquet Sauce and Melted Butter	Hamburgers, Beef, Lamb, Pork, Poultry	Brush on meat; rub into poultry
Worcestershire or Steak Sauce and Water	Hamburgers, Beef, Lamb, Pork	Brush on
Onion Soup or Gravy Mix, Bouillon Granules	Hamburgers, Beef, Lamb	Sprinkle on before microwaving
Taco Seasoning Mix	Hamburgers, Savory Quick Breads	Sprinkle on before microwaving
Jelly, Preserves or Glazes	Ham, Poultry	Glaze ham during the last 10 minutes or after microwaving; poultry after ½ cooking time

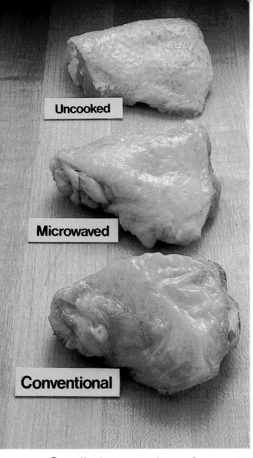

Uncooked

Microwaved

Conventional

Small pieces and non-fatty cuts do not brown because there is no caramelization of fat. They do change color and look cooked.

Lay strips of bacon over a meatloaf or roast. Bacon bastes and flavors meat, which browns under the bacon. When the meat is done, the bacon will be cooked but not brown, because the surface of the meat lowers its temperature below the point where color develops.

Use bouquet sauce mixtures only for small or non-fatty cuts, and apply it sparingly to achieve the degree of color you prefer. Dry poultry well and rub the mixture into the skin. Because poultry skin is very fatty, sauce may bead up or streak if brushed on.

Microwave steaks on a browning utensil to obtain the carbonized color and flavor associated with this type of beef.

Testing Meat for Doneness

Standing time is important in meat microwaving. It is part of the cooking process and should never be omitted. During standing meat continues to cook and tenderize. Wait until standing is completed to test for doneness; microwave longer if necessary.

Tests for doneness vary with the type of meat and cooking method used. Look at the meat and touch it to determine doneness. Except for poultry, the most accurate test for large, tender roasts is internal temperature. Use a microwave thermometer or an automatic temperature probe, if your oven is equipped with one.

The thermometer can be inserted before roast is placed in oven. Since the first half of cooking is done by time, a temperature probe should be inserted when the roast is turned over and the oven is set to cook by temperature. A conventional meat thermometer may be used outside of the oven but should be removed during microwaving.

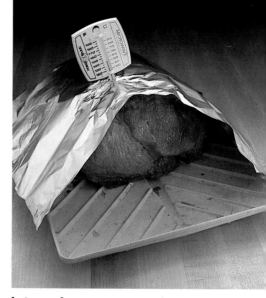

Internal temperature of tender roasts rises 10° to 15° during standing. Tent loosely with foil, shiny side in. Do not cover tightly or it will taste steamed.

How to Test Beef and Lamb

Internal temperature of tender beef and lamb roasts depends upon the doneness. Allow for a temperature rise on standing.

Less tender cuts darken in color, are fork tender and split at the fibers. Appearance and feel of tender steaks and chops varies with doneness desired. See page 24.

How to Test Pork

Internal temperature of pork roasts should be about 165° on removal from the oven and will rise to 170° on standing.

Pierce meat with a knife. It should feel tender but firm. Fibers will not separate as they do for less tender cuts of beef.

Color of cooked meat will be light. Juices should be slightly pink. Tests show pork needs less cooking than was formerly believed safe.

Pork, veal and poultry should be cooked well done but they toughen and dry out rapidly if overcooked. Standing time allows them to complete cooking and remain juicy. Tent loosely with foil, shiny side in.

Less tender cuts require standing time to soften the fibers. Keep them tightly covered to hold in steam which tenderizes meat.

How to Test Veal

Microwave veal to an internal temperature of 160°. It will rise to 165° to 170° on standing. Standing time tenderizes veal.

Fully cooked veal is fork tender but firm to the touch. It will be light grey in color. Because it contains very little fat, veal toughens and dries out if it is overcooked.

How to Test Poultry

Do not use an automatic temperature probe. Hot melted fat runs along the probe and may turn the oven off before the bird is done.

Move drumstick up and down; joint should give readily. Flesh feels soft when pinched.

Cut between inner thigh and breast or next to thigh bone. Meat should show no pink and juices should run clear.

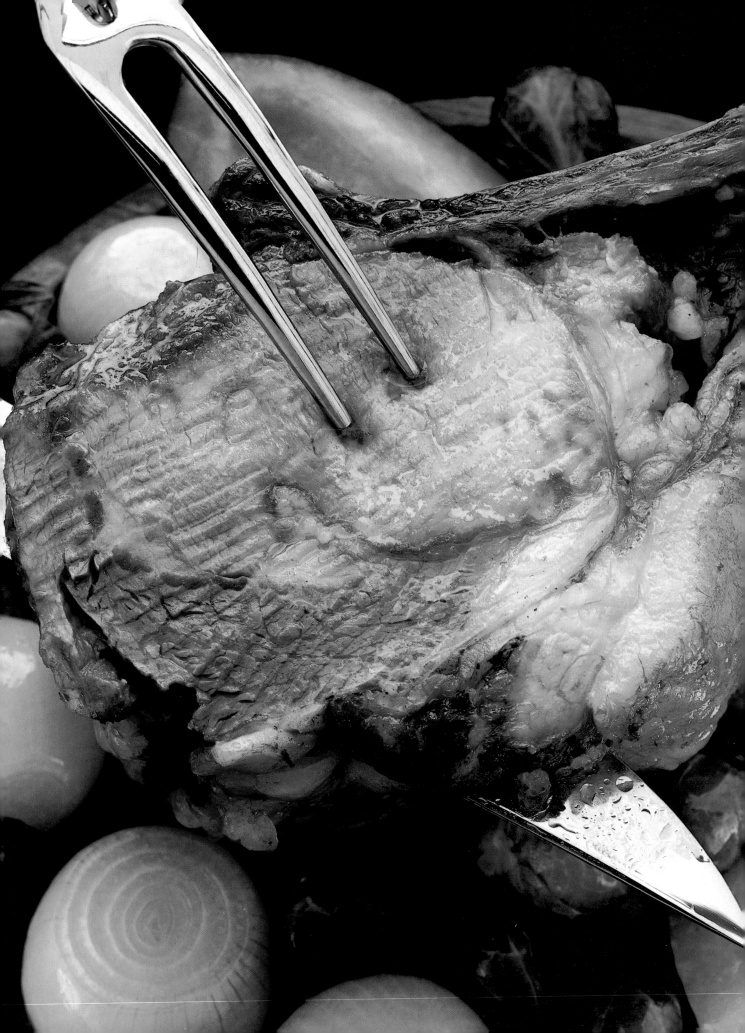

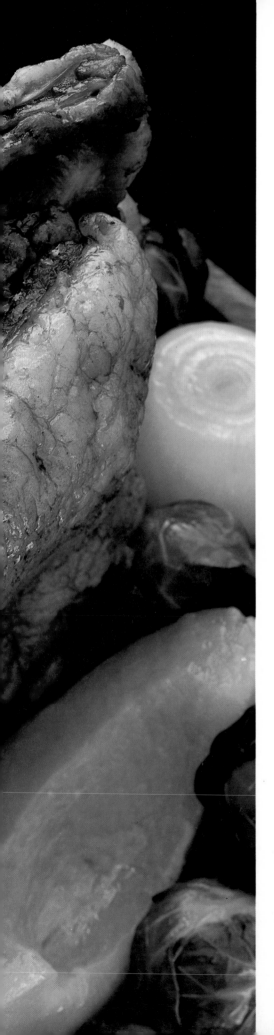

Beef

Beef is America's most popular meat. Much of it is also expensive. If you choose it wisely, store it carefully and cook it appropriately, microwaved beef will be more tender and juicy than conventionally cooked. Poor storage and cooking by any method will spoil beef.

Microwaving is faster than conventional cooking, but the methods used are the same. Tender beef is dry roasted or grilled on a browning utensil. Less tender beef should be microwave-braised or stewed to develop tenderness and flavor. If you are in doubt about the cooking method, be guided by your conventional experience.

Consult your butcher if you are a beginning cook, or have moved to a new part of the country. (Beef varies from one region to another.) Supermarkets have butchers who can be summoned by the ring of a bell and will tell you from which wholesale cut the meat was taken, whether it is choice or good grade, corn or grass-fed. He may even advise you how to cook it.

All these questions are a guide to cooking methods. Even without the butcher, this book tells you how to judge, choose, store and cook beef. Remember that you needn't buy a tender cut of beef to have tender meat, you only need to microwave it wisely.

Know Your Beef

Two factors determine the appropriate method for cooking a piece of beef. These are the grade of beef and the cut selected.

Most beef available in supermarkets is either Choice Grade or Good Grade, sometimes sold as "economy beef". The quality of beef available may depend on the region in which you live. In some parts of the country, cattle are entirely grass-fed. Range-fed cattle exercise as they browse. They develop little fat and their muscles become tough and stringy. In other regions cattle are confined in feeder lots where they are fattened on corn. Fat around and within the muscles makes meat tender and flavorful.

Choice beef has a good covering of firm fat and thin veins of fat, called marbling, within the lean meat.

Good beef has a thinner covering of fat, which may be somewhat soft or oily. There may be some marbling.

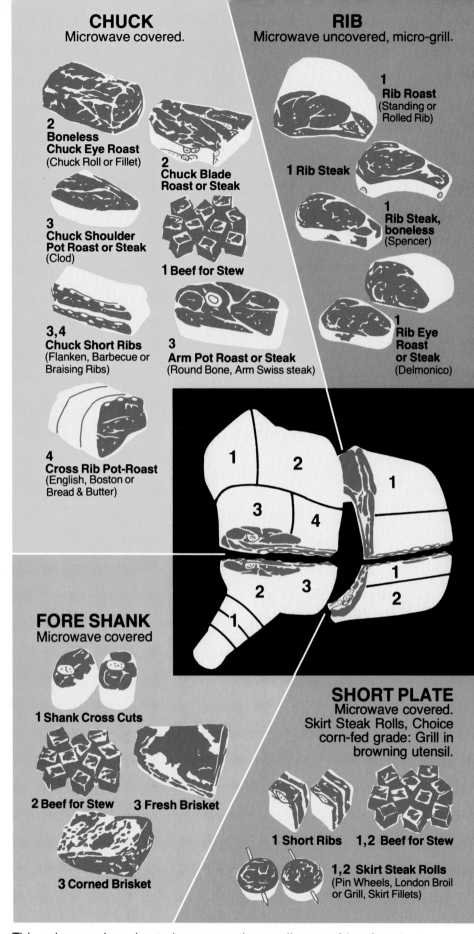

CHUCK
Microwave covered.

2 Boneless Chuck Eye Roast (Chuck Roll or Fillet)

2 Chuck Blade Roast or Steak

3 Chuck Shoulder Pot Roast or Steak (Clod)

1 Beef for Stew

3,4 Chuck Short Ribs (Flanken, Barbecue or Braising Ribs)

3 Arm Pot Roast or Steak (Round Bone, Arm Swiss steak)

4 Cross Rib Pot-Roast (English, Boston or Bread & Butter)

RIB
Microwave uncovered, micro-grill.

1 Rib Roast (Standing or Rolled Rib)

1 Rib Steak

1 Rib Steak, boneless (Spencer)

1 Rib Eye Roast or Steak (Delmonico)

FORE SHANK
Microwave covered

1 Shank Cross Cuts

2 Beef for Stew   **3 Fresh Brisket**

3 Corned Brisket

SHORT PLATE
Microwave covered.
Skirt Steak Rolls, Choice corn-fed grade: Grill in browning utensil.

1 Short Ribs   **1,2 Beef for Stew**

1,2 Skirt Steak Rolls (Pin Wheels, London Broil or Grill, Skirt Fillets)

This microwaving chart shows popular retail cuts of beef and the wholesale cuts from which they are taken, based on standards set by the National Livestock and Meat Board. Ground

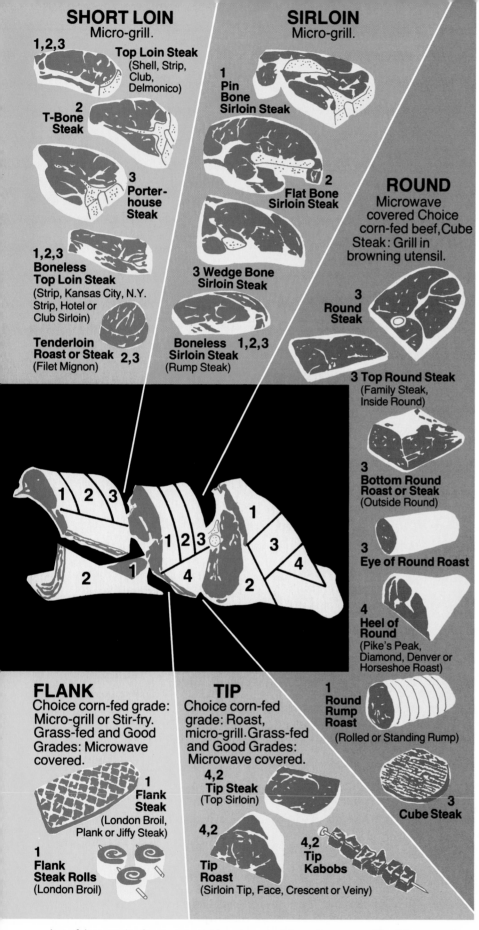

SHORT LOIN
Micro-grill.

1,2,3 **Top Loin Steak** (Shell, Strip, Club, Delmonico)

2 **T-Bone Steak**

3 **Porter-house Steak**

1,2,3 **Boneless Top Loin Steak** (Strip, Kansas City, N.Y. Strip, Hotel or Club Sirloin)

Tenderloin Roast or Steak 2,3 (Filet Mignon)

SIRLOIN
Micro-grill.

1 **Pin Bone Sirloin Steak**

2 **Flat Bone Sirloin Steak**

3 **Wedge Bone Sirloin Steak**

Boneless 1,2,3 Sirloin Steak (Rump Steak)

ROUND
Microwave covered Choice corn-fed beef, Cube Steak: Grill in browning utensil.

3 **Round Steak**

3 Top Round Steak (Family Steak, Inside Round)

3 **Bottom Round Roast or Steak** (Outside Round)

3 **Eye of Round Roast**

4 **Heel of Round** (Pike's Peak, Diamond, Denver or Horseshoe Roast)

1 **Round Rump Roast** (Rolled or Standing Rump)

3 **Cube Steak**

FLANK
Choice corn-fed grade: Micro-grill or Stir-fry. Grass-fed and Good Grades: Microwave covered.

1 **Flank Steak** (London Broil, Plank or Jiffy Steak)

1 **Flank Steak Rolls** (London Broil)

TIP
Choice corn-fed grade: Roast, micro-grill. Grass-fed and Good Grades: Microwave covered.

4,2 **Tip Steak** (Top Sirloin)

4,2 **Tip Roast**

4,2 **Tip Kabobs**

(Sirloin Tip, Face, Crescent or Veiny)

The cut of beef is determined by the area from which meat is taken. Even prime and choice cattle have areas, like legs, shoulders and neck, which are well-exercised, and therefore less fat and tender. These cuts must be pot roasted or simmered in liquid. A cut which can be dry roasted or grilled in the choice grade, may need simmering to become tender if it is good grade.

Names for different cuts of beef vary across the country. The National Livestock and Meat Board is attempting to standardize beef terminology. Many markets are adopting the new names; some of them also add the old names to assist consumers in identifying a cut of beef. A piece of meat which you have always called "sirloin tip roast", may now be named "tip round roast", since part of this cut actually comes from the round section, rather than the sirloin.

The recipes in this book employ the standard names. In the chart, we list the standard name and some of the more common regional names. If you are in doubt about a cut of meat, ask your butcher from which wholesale cut it comes. This should indicate the best method of cooking it. If you are uncertain about how to microwave a cut of beef, follow the method you would use conventionally. Tender beef may be dry roasted or grilled in a browning dish, less tender beef should be braised or simmered in liquid.

beef is made from several cuts, and has been omitted because it is easily identified. Retail cuts are given their standard names with common regional names in parenthesis.

Selecting & Storing Beef

Microwaving brings out the natural flavor of meat. When microwaved, quality beef will be juicier and more flavorful than conventionally cooked. However, if the meat has deteriorated through improper storage, microwaving will intensify the "off" flavor of rancid fat.

How to Select Beef

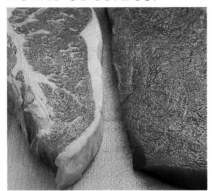

Fat determines the method of microwaving. Well-marbled meat can be dry roasted or cooked on a browning grill. Meat without marbling should be microwaved covered.

Select beef with creamy white, firm and somewhat brittle fat. Avoid fat which is very yellow, soft or oily looking.

Look for firm, velvety, fine-grained flesh and porous red bones. Avoid meat with coarse-grained texture or soft, watery surface. Color may be light to dark red, but should be bright.

How Much Beef to Buy

When buying meat, plan in terms of servings, rather than the number of people served. Three factors determine the amount you will need.

The first is appetite. If you are feeding hearty eaters, increase the portion size or allow for second helpings.

A second factor is the way the meat is served. You will need less meat if it is combined with vegetables, rice or pasta, or is served with several side dishes.

A third, very important factor is the amount of bone and fat in the cut of meat selected. Boneless meat costs more per pound than bone-in, but may be more economical because there is no waste. This is especially true of cuts like rump which have a large proportion of bone. Roasts should weigh at least 3 pounds, or include 2 to 3 ribs. If this is more meat than you need, you will want to plan a meal or two from the leftovers. Pot roasts are cut a minimum of 2 inches thick, but can be divided for several meals.

Boneless Chuck Roast

Bone-in Roast

Buy meat by cost per serving, not per pound. Boneless chuck roast makes three servings per pound; bone-in roast yields two. If the difference in cost per pound is ⅓ or less, boneless meat is your best buy.

Cut	Amount per serving
Boneless steaks and roasts	¼-⅓ pound
Bone-in rib roasts and pot roasts	⅓-½ pound
Round steak	⅓-½ pound
Large steaks	½-¾ pound
Small steaks	1 steak
Cuts with large amounts of fat or bone (rump, short ribs, shanks)	1 pound

How to Store Beef

Refrigerate beef as soon as possible after purchase. Careful covering is important if you have a frost-free refrigerator which circulates dry air. This atmosphere dries out meat and oxygen turns the fat rancid. A marinade will keep meat fresh while tenderizing and flavoring it.

How to Wrap Beef for Refrigerator Storage

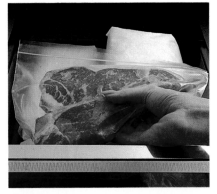

Pre-packaged meat may be stored in the original package but will keep better if you drain the juices, remove the absorbent paper liner and wrap as directed in next picture.

Beef packaged in butcher's paper should be unwrapped. Place meat in a tightly covered dish or wrap loosely in freezer paper, plastic wrap or food storage bag. Cover all sides.

Store beef in or near the meat compartment of your refrigerator. This section is designed to keep meat at the correct temperature and prevent exchange of food odors.

How to Wrap Beef for Freezing

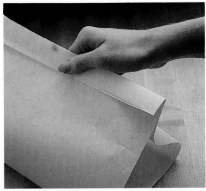

Place meat on unwaxed side of wax-coated freezer paper. Bring edges of paper together and fold over 1-inch.

Fold again; press wrap tightly to beef to force out air. Make as air-tight as possible.

Crease ends of wrap to form triangles. Fold up and seal with continuous strip of freezer tape. Label with cut, number of servings and date of freezing.

Beef Storage Chart

Cut	Refrigerator (40°F.)	Freezer Compartment	Freezer (under −0°)
Large roasts	3-5 days	No more than 1 week, unless you are sure temperature is below 0°. Defrosting times in this book are based on 0° freezer temperature.	6-8 months
Pot roasts	3-5 days		6-8 months
Steaks	3-4 days		6-8 months
Cubed beef	2 days		6-8 months
Cube steaks	2 days		3-4 months
Ground beef	24 hours		3-4 months

How to Take Advantage of Good Beef Buys

Many supermarkets feature a cut of beef as a weekly special. If these cuts are too large for your family you can still take advantage of the saving without eating leftovers day after day. Cut up the meat as suggested here, and cook it in different ways for several days, or freeze it for future use.

How to Divide an Arm (Round Bone) Pot-Roast

Cut a piece from round end or side of roast, depending on position of bone. Cube this meat for beef stew.

Use the section with bone for a small pot roast.

Split the end of the roast into 2 pieces for Swiss steak.

How to Divide a Tip Roast (Choice Grade)

Select a choice grade roast which can be microwaved like tender beef. This cut is often called "sirloin tip" because it extends from the sirloin to the round section. Make 2 smaller roasts, or slice some of the meat into 1 to 1½-in. steaks.

Cube the tail of the roast, which contains some sinews, for kabobs, or slice in strips for stir-fries and ragouts.

How to Cut up a Chuck Steak

Chuck steak is a good buy for one person, since each steak can be divided to make 2 to 3 meals. Locate the butterfly bones at the pointed end of the steak.

Cut away this tender area, which is an extension of the rib section. Microwave it in a browning dish like a rib steak.

Tenderize and microwave the remaining meat as you would any less tender steak, or cube the meat for beef stew.

How to Trim Beef Tenderloin

The tenderloin section of cattle is so little exercised that it is tender in any grade of beef. It is surrounded by a membrane and a tough fibrous tissue which must be removed before it is cooked. Much of the cost of tenderloin is due to this labor, so many supermarkets offer untrimmed tenderloins at great savings. If you plan to freeze part of the meat, ask the butcher if it has been frozen, or buy a frozen piece. Partially frozen tenderloin is easy to trim and cut, and may be refrozen if there are still ice crystals present in the meat.

Remove fat and membrane. Lift a strip of the fibrous tissue with a sharp knife.

Hold strip in one hand and peel it off, scraping with knife held against the fibers so no meat is removed.

Locate and remove the tendon on the outside of the small muscle, using the knife to scrape as you pull.

How to Divide Beef Tenderloin

Halve tenderloin to make two roasts. Fold thin end back against meat and tie in place for an even roast.

Slice meat, if it is not needed for roasts, into 1 to 2-in. steaks. Freeze as directed for ground beef patties.

Cube the thin end of tenderloin for kabobs or cut in strips for stir-fries or sautés.

How to Re-package Bulk Ground Beef

Shape beef into patties on cookie sheet. Freeze until firm. Seal in heavy plastic bag or wrap in freezer paper.

Divide beef into 1 to 1½-pound packages for use in meatloaves or balls. Make a depression in the center of meat to give it a ring shape for easy defrosting.

Microwave crumbled ground beef until it loses its pink color. Cool, and package recipe-size amounts in shallow freezer boxes for use in casseroles.

Defrosting Beef

Proper freezing and careful defrosting retain the quality of beef. Unwrapping the meat speeds defrosting. The plastic tray used for pre-packaged beef insulates the meat, while juices absorbed by the paper liner will draw microwave energy.

Frozen meat begins to loose juices as it defrosts. Elevate the meat on a roasting rack or inverted saucer so juices in the dish cannot cause surface cooking. Be sure to shield warm areas.

How to Defrost Roasts Over 2-inches Thick

Rib, Rump, Tip & Eye of Round

50% (Medium) 5½-6½ min. per lb.
30% (Low) 8½-12½ min. per lb.

Place plastic or paper-wrapped package in oven. Defrost for ¼ the total time.

Remove all packaging, including spice packet from corned beef. Place rack or inverted saucer in baking dish.

Feel roast for warm areas and shield these with foil. Turn roast over onto rack or saucer.

How to Defrost Tenderloin, Flat Roasts & Large Steaks

50% (Medium) 3½-4½ min. per lb.
30% (Low) 7-9 min. per lb.

Place package in oven. Defrost for half the time. Remove wrapping, tray and liner.

Shield any warm areas with foil. Turn meat over onto rack or inverted saucer. Defrost remaining time.

Let stand 5 minutes. When meat can be pierced to center with fork, it is defrosted.

Greatest loss of juices occurs after defrosting. One advantage of a microwave oven is that you can defrost meat just before cooking and reduce the amount of moisture loss. Keep the meat solidly frozen until you place it in the oven. If you like rare roast beef, let the meat stand only 15 to 20 minutes and begin cooking while you can still feel ice crystals in the center when a skewer is inserted.

Corned Beef

50% (Medium) 6-8 min. per lb.
30% (Low) 11-13 min. per lb.

Defrost for second ¼ of time, or until surface yields to pressure. Turn over; let stand 10 minutes.

Defrost for third ¼ of time. Shield warm areas; turn roast over. Defrost remaining time.

Let stand 20 to 30 minutes, or until a skewer can be inserted to the center of roast.

How to Defrost Small Steaks

50% (Medium) 3-4 min. per lb.
30% (Low) 5½-7 min. per lb.

Remove as much wrapping as possible. Separate steaks with table knife, if stacked. Arrange on rack.

Defrost for half the total time. Remove any remaining wrapping. Turn steaks over.

Defrost for second half of time. Let stand 5 minutes, or until steaks can be pierced to the center.

How to Defrost Beef Ribs

50% (Medium) 3-6 min. per lb.
30% (Low) 5-10 min. per lb.

Unwrap ribs. Place on rack in baking dish. Defrost for half the total time. Separate ribs.

Arrange ribs with least defrosted parts to outside of dish. Defrost remaining time, or until skewer can be inserted, but some ice crystals remain in center.

Let stand 10 to 15 minutes, until a skewer can be inserted to the bone easily.

How to Defrost Ground Beef

50% Power (Medium) 3¾-4¾ minutes per lb.
30% Power (Low) 5-7 minutes per lb.

Place paper or plastic package in oven. Defrost for ⅓ of time.

Turn package over. Defrost for second ⅓ of time.

Open package. Scrape off and remove soft pieces. Set aside.

How to Defrost Cubes and Strips

Place package in oven. Defrost for half the total time. Unwrap and separate pieces, removing any which are defrosted.

Spread meat in baking dish. Defrost remaining time, or until surface is soft to the touch.

Let stand 5 to 10 minutes, or until a fork can be inserted to center of meat.

Place remaining meat in casserole. Break up with fork. Defrost remaining time.

Interrupt defrosting of amounts over 1-lb. part way through last period to remove soft pieces.

Let stand 5 minutes (1-lb.) to 10 minutes (over 1-lb.) until meat is softened but still icy.

23

Testing Beef for Doneness

Rare. Remove roast from the oven at 120°. If carved immediately, meat is very rare. During standing, roast continues to cook and internal temperature rises to 140°.

Roasts

The most accurate way to determine the doneness of roast beef is with a microwave thermometer or probe which registers internal temperature. Minutes per pound help you estimate how long the roast will take to cook, but can only be approximate. Roasts of the same weight differ in thickness, shape and amount of fat, and microwave ovens vary in cooking speed.

Whether you roast beef conventionally or by microwave, the meat should stand after removal from the oven. This allows the juices to settle while the meat firms up for carving. During this time the meat continues to cook.

Many conventional cookbooks recommend internal temperatures which are not only higher than restaurant beef, but do not allow for this additional cooking. If you roast beef to 140°, often suggested for rare, the internal temperature will rise to 155° or 160° before serving. That's medium. To avoid disappointment, remove the roast from the oven when the internal temperature is 10° to 20° lower than the finished temperature desired.

How to Use the Internal Temperatures in this Book

This book indicates the internal temperature at which you should remove beef from the oven, rather than the finished temperature. These pictures illustrate the changes in appearance and temperature which occur during standing time. In each, the roast above was carved immediately after microwaving while the roast below was allowed to stand 10 minutes.

Steaks and Hamburgers

Tender steaks are microwaved to the doneness preferred and served immediately without standing time. In addition to the sight and touch tests given opposite, bone-in steaks may be tested by inserting a knife between bone and meat observing the color. These tests also apply to hamburgers and lamb chops.

Less Tender Beef

Less tender beef is done when it is fork tender and splits at the fibers. Color of the meat will be brown. After microwaving less tender beef, let it stand tightly covered to complete tenderizing.

Rare. Steak is well-browned but no juices appear on the surface. Meat gives easily when touched.

Medium-rare. Roast is removed from the oven at 125°. It looks rare, but will cook to 145° when allowed to stand.

Medium. Microwave roast to 135°. If carved immediately, center will still be pink. After standing, temperature is 150°.

Well. Remove the roast from the oven at 150°. It will appear medium-done. Temperature rises to 160°, only 10° because meat is dryer.

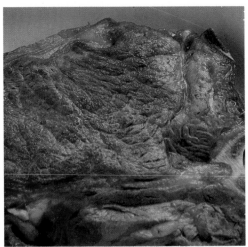

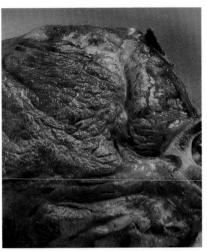

Medium-rare. The moment a drop of juice appears on the the surface of steak, it's ready. Meat is slightly springy and resistant when touched.

Medium. Juices appear on the surface and meat starts to firm.

Well. Juices cover surface, which is firm and does not yield to pressure.

Tender Roasts: Rib

Rolled or standing rib roasts are microwaved uncovered and elevated on a roasting rack or inverted saucers to keep them clear of juices which could produce a steamed or pot-roasted flavor. Minutes per pound are the same for any weight of roast because differences in size are adjusted in the initial cooking at High power. This High power period is part of the first half of cooking time and should be subtracted from it when you determine how long to cook at 50% (Medium) before you stop and turn over roast. If you usually cook Choice Grade Tip Roast like tender beef, you can microwave it following these directions.

Shield tail of standing rib or ends of rolled rib weighing over 5 pounds, to prevent uneven cooking and excessive shrinkage. Remove the foil after ⅔ cooking time.

Rib Roasts

Approx. Total Time: Min./Lb.	Start at High Power	Finish at 50% (Medium)	Remove at Internal Temp.
9-12	Under 4 lbs.	Rare	120°
9½-13	first 5 min.	Medium Rare	125°
10-13½	Over 4 lbs.	Medium	135°
11½-14½	first 8 min.	Well Done	150°

How To Microwave Rib Roasts

Place standing rib or large boneless roast, fat side down, on a rack or inverted saucer set in baking dish. Arrange small boneless roast, cut side up. Smaller roasts do not need shielding. Insert microwave thermometer if used. Estimate total cooking time for desired doneness.

Microwave at High, according to chart above. Reduce power to 50% (Medium). Microwave remaining part of first half of total cooking time.

How to Insert Probe or Thermometer in a Rib Roast

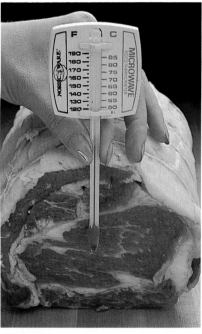

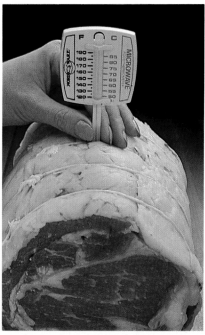

Examine both ends of roast to determine the direction of fat channels or the position of bone. Mirrors demonstrate differences between ends.

Measure the distance from the outside of meat to center of the thickest muscle with your fingers. Mark the point where sensor touches edge of roast.

Insert probe or thermometer to depth marked by your fingers. Select angle which will place tip of sensor in center of meaty area, not touching fat or bone.

Turn roast over so standing rib or large rolled rib are fat side up and small roast has opposite end toward top of oven. This protects ends and makes shielding unnecessary. Insert probe if used. Microwave second half of cooking time or until temperature reaches the removal point for doneness desired.

Remove roast from oven and tent loosely with foil, shiny side in. Do not cover tightly or roast will steam. Let stand 10 minutes.

Insert probe or thermometer at an angle so point reaches center of roast. In a thin roast, angular placement prevents sensor from falling out.

Tender Roasts: Tenderloin

If you purchase an untrimmed tenderloin, see page 19 for directions on how to trim it yourself. The tenderloin tapers toward one end. Fold this thin tip back against the roast to form a uniformly thick, compact shape, and tie it securely. Soft butcher's twine is best, but you can use several twists of dental floss. If the whole tenderloin is too large to fit your dish, halve it and roast both pieces together. Time them according to the total weight, and reverse their position in the oven when rotating dish.

Tenderloin Roasts

Approx. Total Time: Min./Lb.	Start at High Power	Finish at 50% (Medium)	Remove at Internal Temp.
7½-9½	Under 2 lbs.	Rare	120°
8-10	first 3 min.	Medium Rare	125°
9½-11½	Over 2 lbs. first 5 min.	Medium	135°

Filet de Bouef Bouquetiere

Before roasting tenderloin, microwave a selection of miniature vegetables. Use butter for moisture, and undercook slightly. Arrange around outside of microwave-oven safe platter; set aside. Microwave tenderloin. While it is standing, reheat vegetables, then place roast in center. Garnish with parsley sprigs and lemon wedges.

How to Microwave a Tenderloin Roast

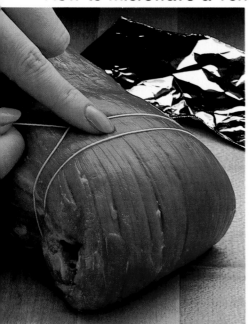

Fold the thin tip under and tie securely to make a uniform, shape. Shield if desired.

Place roast on rack or inverted saucers in baking dish. Insert thermometer if used. Estimate total cooking time.

Microwave at High according to chart above. Reduce power to 50% (Medium). Microwave remaining part of first half of total cooking time.

How & Why to Shield a Tenderloin Roast

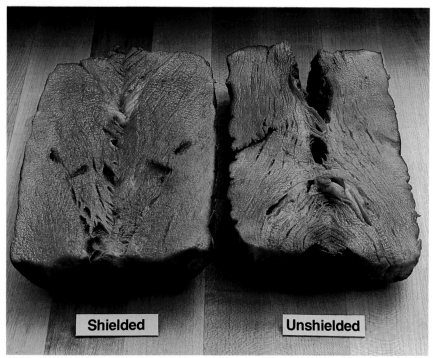

Shielded

Unshielded

Shield roast, if desired, over ends and 1-in. down sides. This reduces shrinkage and moisture loss. Remove foil after ⅔ cooking time.

Shielded roast is uniformly cooked. Every slice is the same. Unshielded roast is more done at ends. This can be desirable if family or guests differ about the degree of doneness prefered.

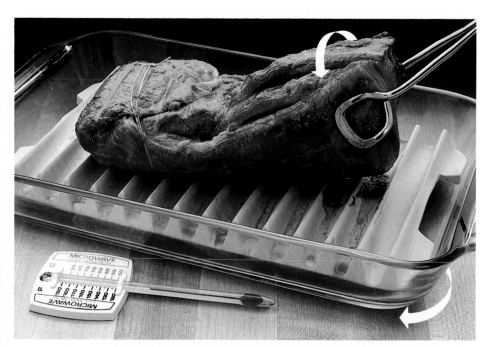

Turn roast over and rotate dish. Insert probe if used. Microwave for second half of cooking time, or until internal temperature reaches the removal point indicated for doneness desired. Remove any shielding after ⅔ cooking time.

Let stand 10 minutes, tented loosely with foil, shiny side in. Temperature will rise 15° to 20°.

Tenderizing Beef

Less tender cuts and grades of beef contain little marbling to break up the long, tough fibers. They must be braised or cooked in liquid to make them tender. In addition, there are several natural methods of tenderizing which you can use before cooking. If you prefer to use a chemical tenderizer, select one which is not seasoned. Microwaving exaggerates the flavor of seasoned tenderizers.

Some supermarkets sell pre-tendered beef, which has been treated at the packing house with natural enzymes from papaya, pineapple or figs. These enzymes are activated by heat and break down tough tissues. Do not use chemical tenderizers on pretendered beef.

Marinate beef to tenderize and flavor it. A marinade also keeps meat fresh. Several days of marinating in refrigerator will be more effective than a few hours at room temperature.

Pound steaks under 1-in. thick to break up fibers. Use a meat mallet or the edge of a saucer held at right angles to the meat. Springy meat cushions saucer so it won't break. If recipe calls for flour, you may sprinkle it over the meat before pounding; be sure to use a saucer, because the mallet spatters floury juices which adhere like paste.

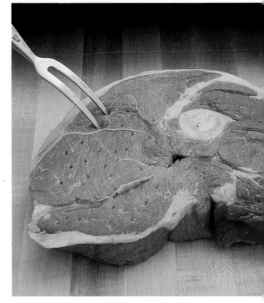

Pierce pot roasts and thick steaks thoroughly with a fork. This enables steam or liquid to reach the interior of the meat during microwaving.

How to Marinate Beef

Combine marinade ingredients in 12×8-in. dish or 3-qt. casserole. Pierce all sides of meat thoroughly with a fork.

Place meat in marinade; cover with plastic wrap. Let stand in refrigerator overnight or several days, or at room temperature 2 to 4 hours.

Turn meat over occasionally. Use marinade for all or part of cooking liquid, except soy marinade, which imparts too strong a flavor and color.

If you're a once-a-week shopper, plan a marinated beef dish for the end of the week. Beef which is placed in a marinade as soon as you bring it home will keep fresh 2 to 3 days longer than unmarinated beef. The marinade need not cover the meat completely, but you should turn meat over at least once a day to keep all surfaces moist. This seals out air and inhibits bacteria growth.

Beer Marinade

1 can (12-oz.) beer
1 medium onion, chopped
½ green pepper, chopped
2 tablespoons Worcestershire sauce
1 bay leaf
½ teaspoon salt
¼ teaspoon pepper
¼ teaspoon tarragon leaves

Makes about 2½ cups

Mix all ingredients together well.

Soy Marinade

½ cup soy sauce
2 tablespoons Worcestershire sauce
2 tablespoons lemon juice
¼ teaspoon pepper
⅛ teaspoon ground ginger

Makes about ¾ cup

Mix all ingredients together well.

Tomato Marinade

1 can (8-oz.) tomato sauce
2 tablespoons brown sugar
1 medium onion, chopped
1 clove garlic, minced or pressed
1 teaspoon parsley flakes
½ teaspoon basil, crushed
½ teaspoon oregano, crushed

Makes about 1¾ cups

Stir tomato sauce and brown sugar together until smooth. Add remaining ingredients; mix well.

Savory Wine Marinade

1½ cups red or white wine
¼ cup wine vinegar
2 tablespoons oil
3 cloves garlic, peeled and halved
1 medium onion, sliced
1 medium carrot, sliced
1 teaspoon salt
½ teaspoon oregano or basil, crushed
½ teaspoon marjoram or thyme, crushed
⅛ teaspoon pepper

Makes about 3 cups

Mix all ingredients together well.

Quick Wine Marinade

1 cup red wine
½ cup water
2 tablespoons parsley flakes
2 teaspoons oregano
2 teaspoons basil
½ teaspoon salt
¼ teaspoon thyme

Mix all ingredients together well.

Less Tender Roasts

In conventional cooking, less tender cuts of beef are braised or cooked in liquid. These techniques differ only in the amount of moisture added. Less liquid is needed for microwaving, because there is little evaporation. Sometimes chopped onion or celery produce sufficient moisture.

Use a tight cover to hold in steam. If your casserole lid does not fit tightly, lay a sheet of wax paper or plastic wrap between dish and lid for a snug fit.

Slower cooking tenderizes meat. At 50% (Medium) the roast will cook faster but be more chewy than at 30% (Low). Meat should be microwaved until it is fork tender and splits at the fibers, then allowed to stand. Standing time is essential. It completes tenderizing and allows flavors to blend.

How to Microwave Less Tender Beef Roasts

Pierce meat deeply and thoroughly with a long-tined fork. For added tenderness and flavor, marinate several hours or overnight.

Place meat and liquid in casserole, baking dish or bag. Cover dishes tightly. Tie bag loosely with plastic strip, leaving a small space for steam to escape. Place bag in baking dish.

32

Fruited Pot Roast

2 to 3½ lb. top round steak, cut 1½-in. thick
¼ cup plus 1 tablespoon orange juice
2 tablespoons barbecue sauce
1 tablespoon soy sauce
1 teaspoon grated orange peel
½ teaspoon salt
1 can (4-oz.) mushroom stems and pieces, drained
1 medium onion, sliced
¼ cup cold water
1½ tablespoons cornstarch
1 to 2 tablespoons brown sugar
1 medium orange, sliced

Serves 6 to 8

Pierce both sides of meat thoroughly with a fork. Place in 3-qt. casserole.

In a 2-cup measure combine orange juice, barbecue sauce, soy sauce, orange peel and salt. Pour over meat. Add mushrooms and onion. Cover tightly. Microwave at 50% (Medium) 25 to 30 minutes per pound, or until meat is fork tender, turning roast over halfway through cooking.

Mix water, cornstarch and sugar together in a 2 cup measure until smooth. Add enough meat drippings to equal 1¼ cups. Set aside.

Place orange slices on top of meat. Cover; let stand 8 minutes. Microwave cornstarch mixture at High 2 to 3 minutes, or until thickened, stirring once. Stir into remaining juices around meat. To serve, slice meat thinly across the grain.

To microwave at 30% (Low), increase cooking time to 45 to 50 minutes per pound.

Variation:
Substitute lemon peel for orange peel, ¼ cup water plus 1 tablespoon lemon juice for orange juice and 2 sliced lemons for the sliced orange.

Microwave at 50% (Medium) for half the time. Turn roast over. Add vegetables if called for in recipe. Cover or reseal. Microwave remaining time.

Let roast stand, tightly covered, 20 to 30 minutes to complete tenderizing and improve flavor.

◄ Swedish Pot Roast

2½ to 3½ lb. sirloin tip roast
  2 medium onions, sliced
  2 tablespoons cider vinegar
  2 tablespoons dark corn syrup
  2 bay leaves
  2 teaspoons salt

½ teaspoon ground allspice
½ teaspoon pepper

Gravy:
  ¼ cup cold water
  ¼ cup flour
  1 cup whipping cream

Serves 6 to 8

Pierce meat thoroughly with a fork. Place roast, onions, vinegar, corn syrup and seasonings in 3-qt. casserole. Cover tightly. Microwave at 50% (Medium) 25 to 30 minutes per pound, or until meat is fork tender, turning roast after half the time. Remove roast from casserole. Tent with foil; let stand while making gravy.

Skim fat from meat drippings, remove bay leaves. Blend water and flour together until smooth. Stir into drippings. Microwave at High 3 to 4 minutes, or until thickened, stirring 1 or 2 times. Stir in cream. Reduce power to 50% (Medium). Microwave 1 to 2 minutes, or until heated through. Slice roast thinly across the grain; serve with gravy.

To microwave at 30% (Low), increase cooking time to 40 to 50 minutes per pound.

Braised Rump Roast

3 to 4 lb. boneless rump roast
½ cup hot water
2 teaspoons instant beef
  bouillon

1 tablespoon Worcestershire
  sauce
2 large stalks celery, halved
1 medium onion cut in eighths

Serves 8 to 12

Pierce meat thoroughly with fork. Place in cooking bag. Add water, bouillon and Worcestershire sauce. Close bag loosely, tying with strip cut from end of bag. Microwave at 50% (Medium) 35 minutes.

Turn roast over. Add vegetables. Reclose bag. Microwave 35 to 45 minutes, or until meat is fork tender. Let stand in bag 10 minutes before serving. Slice meat thinly across grain; serve with cooking juices.

To microwave at 30% (Low), increase cooking times to 60 minutes and 60 to 70 minutes.

◄ Barbecued Beef Roast

2½ to 3½ lb. eye of round roast,
  trimmed of excess fat

1½ cups barbecue sauce

Serves 6 to 8

Pierce meat thoroughly with fork. Place in cooking bag; add sauce. Close bag loosely with strip cut from end of bag. Marinate at room temperature 3 to 4 hours or overnight in refrigerator.

Set bag in shallow dish. Microwave at 50% (Medium) 20 to 25 minutes per pound, until meat is tender, turning over after half the time. Let stand, in bag, 10 minutes. Slice thinly across grain.

To microwave at 30% (Low), increase cooking time to 35 to 40 minutes per pound.

Belgian Pot Roast

This cooking technique flavors the meat very subtly. For increased flavor, combine all ingredients in bag and marinate 3 to 4 hours at room temperature or overnight in the refrigerator.

2 to 3 lb. eye of round roast, trimmed of excess fat
½ teaspoon ground thyme
1 teaspoon salt
¼ to ½ teaspoon pepper
1 medium bay leaf
1 can (12-oz.) beer

Serves 6 to 8

Pierce all surfaces of meat thoroughly with a fork. Place roast in cooking bag. Combine seasonings; sprinkle on meat.

Pour beer over roast. Close end of bag loosely, tying with a strip cut from end of bag. Set bag in shallow dish or casserole. Microwave at 50% (Medium) 23 to 28 minutes per pound, or until fork tender, turning meat over halfway through cooking time.

Let stand, in bag, 10 minutes. To serve, slice meat thinly across the grain.

To microwave at 30% (Low), increase cooking time to 40 to 45 minutes per pound.

Sauerbraten ▲

3 to 3½ lb. sirloin tip roast

Marinade:
1¾ cups water
½ cup red wine vinegar
1 medium onion, sliced
1 stalk celery, sliced
1 tablespoon salt
6 whole cloves

4 whole peppercorns
2 bay leaves

Gravy:
Reserved strained marinade
¼ cup flour
1 tablespoon brown sugar
10 gingersnaps, crushed

Serves 8 to 10

Mix marinade ingredients together in large bowl or 3-qt. casserole. Add roast. Cover. Marinate in refrigerator 24 to 48 hours, turning roast several times.

Strain marinade. In 3-qt. casserole, place roast and 1 cup strained marinade; preserve remainder for gravy. Cover roast tightly. Microwave at 50% (Medium) 1 hour to 1 hour, 15 minutes, or until meat is fork tender, turning roast over after half the cooking time. Let stand, covered, while making gravy.

Blend flour into reserved strained marinade until smooth. Add brown sugar. Microwave at High 2 to 3 minutes, or until thickened and smooth; stirring every minute.

Place roast on platter. Stir thickened flour mixture into meat drippings. Add gingersnaps. Microwave 1 to 2 minutes at High or until slightly thickened; stirring once.

To microwave at 30% (Low), increase cooking time to 1¾ to 2 hours.

Pot Roast Dinner

2 to 3 lb. chuck roast
1 envelope onion soup mix
¼ cup water
3 medium carrots, cut in half
   lengthwise and into 1 to
   2-in. chunks
2 medium potatoes, peeled
   and cut into eighths

Gravy:
2 tablespoons flour or 1
   tablespoon cornstarch
¼ cup water

Serves 4 to 6

Pierce both sides of meat
thoroughly with a fork. Place in
12×8-in. dish or 3-qt. casserole.

Sprinkle with soup mix. Add
water. Cover tightly. Microwave
at 50% (Medium) 30 minutes.

Turn roast over. Add vegetables.
Cover. Microwave 30 to 45
minutes, or until meat and
vegetables are fork tender. Let
stand, covered, 10 minutes.
Place meat and vegetables in
serving dish and cover.

Skim fat from meat drippings.
Blend flour into water until
smooth. Stir into drippings.
Microwave at High 1½ to 3
minutes, or until thickened,
stirring 1 or 2 times during
cooking. Blend well.

To serve, slice meat thinly
across the grain.

To microwave at 30% (Low),
increase cooking times to 52
minutes and 53 to 68 minutes.

Spiced Pot Roast ▶

2½ to 3 lb. chuck roast
1 cup water
¼ cup soy sauce
2 tablespoons dry sherry
1 medium onion, sliced
1 teaspoon instant beef bouillon
¼ teaspoon ground cinnamon
⅛ teaspoon pepper

2 cups sliced fresh mushrooms
2 medium potatoes, peeled
   and quartered

Gravy:
3 tablespoons cornstarch
¼ cup water
2 cups roast drippings

Serves 4 to 6

Pierce both sides of meat thoroughly with a fork. Place in 3-qt.
casserole with water, soy sauce, sherry, onion, beef bouillon and
seasonings. Cover tightly. Microwave at 50% (Medium) 35 minutes.

Turn roast over. Add mushrooms and potatoes. Re-cover. Microwave 35 to 45 minutes, or until meat is fork tender. Remove 2 cups of
drippings to 1-qt. container. Let roast stand, covered, 10 minutes.

During last 5 minutes of standing time, stir cornstarch and water
together until smooth. Add to drippings in 1-qt. container. Microwave at High 2½ to 3½ minutes, or until thickened.

Slice meat thinly across the grain to serve.

To microwave at 30% (Low), increase cooking times to 1 hour
and 1 to 1¼ hours.

Spanish Pot Roast

2½ to 3½ lb. top roundsteak, cut
   1 to 1½-in. thick
1 medium onion, sliced and
   separated into rings
1 medium green pepper, cut
   into ¾-in. strips
1 clove garlic, minced or
   pressed
1 tablespoon olive oil (optional)

¼ cup red wine or ¼ cup water
   plus 1 teaspoon instant
   beef bouillon
1 can (6-oz.) tomato paste
1 bay leaf
1 teaspoon salt (omit if wine is
   used)
¼ teaspoon pepper
¼ teaspoon sugar
¼ teaspoon basil, crushed

Serves 6 to 8

Pierce both sides of meat thoroughly with a fork. Combine onion,
green pepper, garlic and olive oil in 12×8-in. dish or 3-qt. casserole.
Cover. Microwave at High 1 to 2 minutes or until vegetables are
tender-crisp. Push to sides of dish.

Place meat in casserole. Top with vegetables. In a 2-cup measure,
stir remaining ingredients together. Pour over meat. Cover tightly.
Reduce power to 50% (Medium). Microwave 30 minutes.

Turn meat over. Spoon sauce over surface. Cover. Microwave 30 to
45 minutes, or until meat is fork tender. Let stand, covered, 5 to 10
minutes. Slice roast thinly across the grain and serve with sauce.

To microwave at 30% (Low), increase cooking times to 52 minutes
and 53 to 68 minutes.

Chuck Roast With Mushroom Sauce

2½ to 3 lb. chuck roast
1 can (10¾-oz.) cream
  of mushroom soup
1 tablespoon Worcestershire
  sauce
2 teaspoons parsley flakes

½ teaspoon salt
⅛ to ¼ teaspoon pepper
⅛ teaspoon garlic powder or 1
  clove garlic, minced
1 cup dairy sour cream

Serves 4 to 6

Pierce both sides of meat thoroughly with a fork. Place roast into a 2 to 2½-qt. casserole or utility dish. In a small bowl, combine remaining ingredients except sour cream. Pour over meat. Cover tightly. Microwave at 50% (Medium) 65 to 75 minutes, or until meat is fork tender, turning roast over after half the cooking time. Let stand, covered, 10 minutes.

Remove meat from casserole. Set aside. Stir sour cream with meat drippings until smooth. If necessary, microwave at 50% (Medium) 4 to 6 minutes to reheat. Slice roast thinly across the grain. Place slices in sour cream sauce to serve.

To microwave at 30% (Low), increase cooking time to 1¾ to 2 hours.

How To Carve Blade Roast

Cut out bones with sharp knife. Separate main muscles. Direction of grain is different in each muscle. Carve separately, directly across the grain, for greatest tenderness.

New England Boiled Dinner ▶

2½ to 3 lb. corned beef round or brisket with seasoning packet
1½ cups water
3 medium carrots, peeled and cut into thin strips
2 large unpeeled potatoes, cut into eighths
1 medium head cabbage, cut into sixths

Serves 6 to 8

Place corned beef, contents of seasoning packet, water and carrots in 3-qt. casserole. Cover tightly. Microwave at High 7 to 9 minutes or until water boils.

Reduce power to 50% (Medium). Microwave 30 minutes.

Turn meat over. Add potatoes and top with cabbage. Re-cover. Microwave 30 to 45 minutes, or until vegetables are tender, rotating dish ½ turn after half the cooking time.

Let stand, covered, 10 minutes. To serve, carve corned beef diagonally across the grain in thin slices.

To microwave at 30% (Low), increase cooking times to 40 minutes and 40 to 80 minutes.

Carve brisket and corned beef diagonally across the grain in thin slices. Cutting across the grain shortens fibers.

Glazed Corned Beef

3 lb. corned beef round or brisket with seasoning packet
2 cups water

Glaze:
¼ cup brown sugar
1 tablespoon prepared mustard
Dash nutmeg

Serves 8 to 10

Place corned beef, contents of seasoning packet and water in 2-qt. casserole. Cover tightly. Microwave at High 7 to 9 minutes or until water starts to boil.

Reduce power to 50% (Medium). Microwave 18 to 22 minutes per pound, turning meat over after half the cooking time. Let stand in liquid, covered, for 15 minutes.

Mix all glaze ingredients together in small bowl. Microwave at High ½ to 1 minute, or until brown sugar melts.

Remove corned beef from liquid. Spoon glaze over meat. To serve, carve diagonally across the grain in thin slices.

To microwave at 30% (Low), increase cooking time to 30 to 36 minutes per pound.

How to Microwave in a Clay Pot

Soak pot and lid in water as manufacturer directs. Drain, but do not dry.

Place meat in pot, fat side down. Add other ingredients as directed in recipe. Cover.

Microwave as directed in recipe, turning meat once or twice during cooking, keeping vegetables on top of meat.

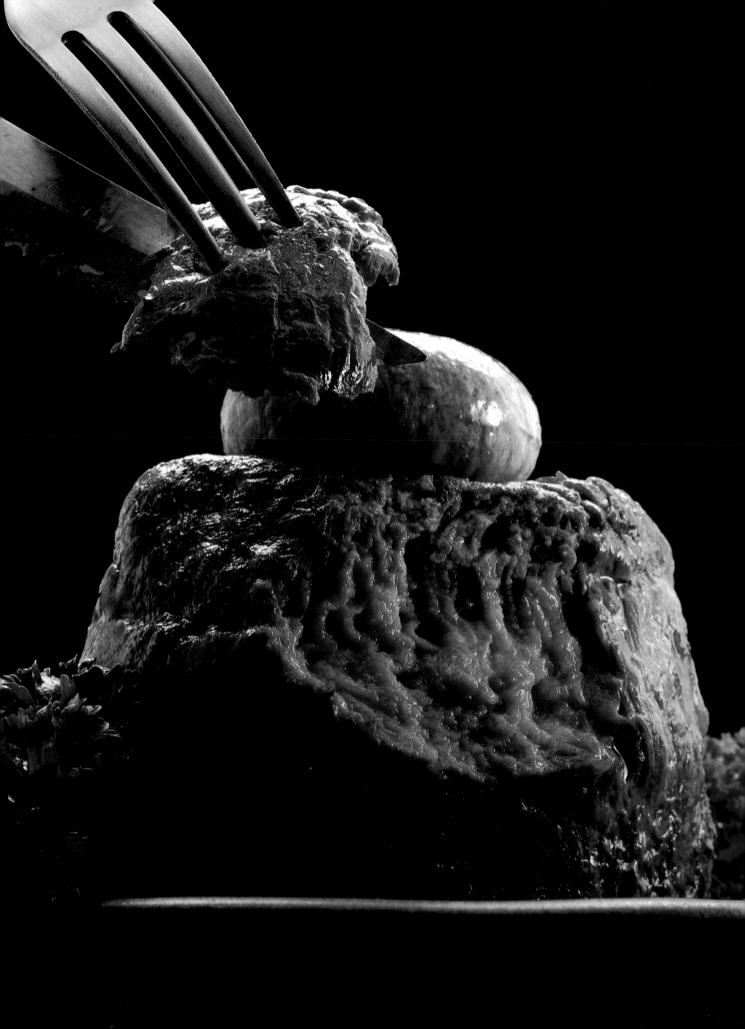

Tender Steaks

A browning grill or dish gives tender steaks a seared color, surface and flavor. The method for microwaving steaks is similar to conventional cooking, but the time is much shorter. Conventionally a rare steak, 1½-inches thick, will take from 10 to 30 minutes in a pre-heated broiler or fry pan. In a pre-heated browning utensil, it microwaves in 3 to 4 minutes.

How To Microwave Steaks In Browning Utensil

Preheat browning dish or grill as manufacturer directs. Slash fatty rim of steak at 1-in. intervals to prevent curling.

Place steak on grill. Microwave the first side at High Power. Do not salt steak until after cooking.

Turn steak over. Microwave second side. See page 24 for tests for doneness.

Tender Steak Chart

High Power	Rare		Medium Rare		Medium		Well	
	1st side	2nd side	1st side	2nd side	1st side	2nd side	1st side	2nd side
No. of Steaks	Minutes	Minutes	Minutes	Minutes	Minutes	Minutes	Minutes	Minutes
1 steak, 1-in. thick	1½	1-1½	1½	1¾-2	2	1¾-2½	2	2¾-3¾
1 steak, 1½-in. thick	1½	1½-1¾	1½	1¾-2¾	2	3-4	2	3¼-4¾
2 steaks, 1½-in. thick	1½	1½-2	1½	2-3	2	3¼-4½	2	4½-5½
4 steaks, 1½-in. thick	2	2-2¾	2	2½-3¼	3	3½-4¾	3	4½-6

Less Tender Steaks

Round Steak Roll-ups

2 to 2½-lb. round steak, ½-in. thick

Stuffing:
2 cups sliced fresh mushrooms, divided
½ cup chopped onion
¼ cup chopped celery
⅓ cup water
2 tablespoons butter or margarine
1 teaspoon parsley flakes
½ teaspoon salt
⅛ teaspoon pepper
⅛ teaspoon ground thyme
⅛ teaspoon ground sage
4 slices bread, cubed

Gravy:
¼ cup flour
1 cup water, divided
2 teaspoons instant beef bouillon
1 teaspoon Worcestershire sauce

Serves 4

Microwave at 50% (Medium) using times given below. To microwave at 30% (Low), increase cooking times to 32 minutes and 33 to 43 minutes.

How to Microwave Round Steak Roll-ups

Cut round steak into 4 rectangles. Pound to ¼-in. thickness with the edge of a saucer or a meat mallet.

Combine 1 cup mushrooms with onion, celery, water and butter in a medium bowl. Microwave at High 3 to 4 minutes or until vegetables are tender-crisp. Stir in seasonings and bread cubes.

Spread equal amounts of stuffing over each piece of round steak, leaving ½-in. border on all sides. Roll pieces, and secure with wooden picks. Set aside.

Creamy Round Steak

1½ lb. round steak, ½-in. thick; pounded to ¼-in. thickness (page 30)
¼ cup flour
1 medium onion, sliced and separated into rings
1 can (10¾-oz.) cream of celery soup
¼ cup mayonnaise or salad dressing
¼ cup milk
1 teaspoon Worcestershire sauce
1 clove garlic, minced or pressed

Serves 4 to 6

Dredge steak in flour and place in 12×8-in. baking dish. Top with onion slices.

Combine remaining ingredients; pour over steak. Cover. Microwave at 50% (Medium) 25 minutes.

Turn over and rearrange meat. Baste with sauce. Re-cover. Microwave 20 to 30 minutes, or until meat is fork tender.

Let stand 10 minutes.

Swiss Steak

1½ to 2½ lbs. round steak, cut in serving size pieces
¼ to ⅓ cup flour
½ teaspoon salt
¼ teaspoon pepper
1 can (16-oz.) whole tomatoes in juice
¼ cup chopped onion
1 teaspoon parsley flakes

Serves 4 to 6

Pound meat with edge of saucer or meat mallet to flatten it to ¼ to ½-in. thickness.

Measure flour, salt and pepper into paper bag. Place meat in bag and shake to coat with seasoned flour.

Arrange meat in a 12×8-in. dish, sprinkle any remaining flour over it. Combine tomatoes, onion and parsley flakes; pour over meat. Cover tightly. Microwave at 50% (Medium) 25 minutes.

Turn over and rearrange meat. Re-cover. Microwave 25 to 35 minutes, or until meat is fork tender. Let stand tightly covered 10 minutes.

To microwave at 30% (Low), increase cooking times to 42 minutes and 45 to 60 minutes.

Saucy Cube Steaks

4 beef cubed steaks, 5-oz. each
2 cups sliced fresh mushrooms
½ cup thinly sliced onion
2 tablespoons flour
¼ teaspoon salt
⅛ teaspoon pepper
1 teaspoon parsley flakes
1 cup milk
1 cup shredded cheddar cheese

Serves 4

Arrange cube steaks in 12×7-in. dish. Cover with wax paper. Microwave at High 4 minutes.

Turn steaks over. Cover; rotate dish ½ turn. Microwave 2 to 3 minutes. Meat will still have a slightly pink interior. Remove meat from dish and set aside, covered loosely with foil.

Drain all but 2 to 3 tablespoons drippings from dish. Add mushrooms and onion. Cover with wax paper. Microwave 1½ to 2½ minutes or until tender.

Blend in flour and seasonings. Slowly stir in milk. Microwave 4 to 6 minutes or until thickened. Add cheese. Return steaks to dish; spoon sauce over them. Microwave 1 minute.

Blend flour and ¼ cup water together until smooth in a 2-qt. casserole. Add remaining water, bouillon and Worcestershire sauce. Microwave at High 2½ to 3½ minutes or until thickened, stirring once.

Arrange beef rolls in casserole, seam side up. Spoon gravy over rolls. Cover tightly. Reduce power to 50% (Medium). Microwave 20 minutes.

Turn rolls over and add remaining mushrooms. Re-cover. Microwave 20 to 25 minutes, or until meat is fork tender. Let stand, covered, 10 minutes before serving.

Beef Strips

Strips made from both tender and less tender beef will be more tender if cut correctly.

Beef Bourguignonne

Round steak can be substituted for sirloin if you increase the cooking time. Microwave at 50% (Medium) 55 to 65 minutes, or at 30% (Low) 1½ to 1¾ hours.

  4 slices bacon, quartered
1½ to 2 lb. sirloin steak cut in
        ¼-in. wide strips
  ⅓ cup flour
  ½ lb. fresh mushrooms, sliced
  4 small onions, cut into sixths
  1 medium carrot, chopped
  1 clove garlic, minced or
        pressed
  1 cup burgundy wine
  ½ cup water
  1 tablespoon parsley flakes
  2 teaspoons instant beef
        bouillon
  1 teaspoon salt
  ½ teaspoon thyme, crushed
  ¼ teaspoon pepper
  1 bay leaf

Serves 4 to 6

Place bacon in 3-qt. casserole. Cover. Microwave at High 3 minutes. Drain all but 1 tablespoon drippings.

Stir in steak strips, sprinkle on flour; toss to coat meat evenly. Mix in remaining ingredients. Cover tightly. Microwave at High 5 minutes.

Reduce power to 50% (Medium). Microwave 35 to 45 minutes, or until meat is fork tender and juices are thickened, stirring once after half the cooking time.

Let stand, covered, 10 minutes before serving. Serve over noodles, rice or wild rice.

To microwave at 30% (Low), increase cooking time to 1 to 1¼ hours.

How To Cut Strips

Cut across sirloin, round or tip steaks in ¼-in. strips with the knife parallel to the grain. Divide the strips in 2-in. lengths. Strips are easier to cut from partially frozen beef than from fresh or fully defrosted meat. Choice, corn-fed top round or tip steak can be cooked like tender beef.

◄ Beef Stroganoff

Economical top round steak can be substituted for sirloin if the cooking time is increased. Microwave at 50% (Medium) 55 to 65 minutes or at 30% (Low) 1½ to 1¾ hours.

 1 lb. fresh mushrooms, sliced
 1 large onion, chopped
 2 tablespoons butter or margarine (optional)
1½ to 2 lb. sirloin steak, cut into thin strips
 ¼ cup flour
 2 cups hot water
 1 tablespoon instant beef bouillon
 ½ teaspoon salt
 6 tablespoons tomato paste
 2 teaspoons Worcestershire sauce
 ½ cup dairy sour cream
 1 cup whipping cream

Serves 4 to 6

Combine mushrooms, onion and butter in 3-qt. casserole. Cover. Microwave at High 5½ to 6½ minutes, or until vegetables are tender.

In a small plastic or paper bag, toss meat strips and flour together. Stir meat and flour, water, bouillon and salt into vegetables. Cover. Microwave at High 5 minutes.

Reduce power to 50% (Medium). Microwave 35 to 45 minutes, or until meat is fork tender, stirring halfway through cooking time.

With a wire whip, blend in remaining ingredients until smooth. Serve over rice or noodles.

To microwave at 30% (Low), increase cooking times to 1 hour, 10 minutes to 1 hour, 15 minutes.

TIP: Canned bouillon can be used in place of water and instant bouillon. Dilute as directed on can.

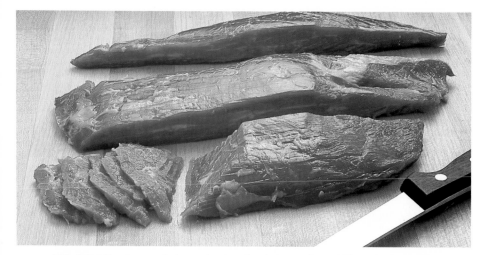

Divide flank steak lengthwise in 2-in. strips. Slice these across the grain in ¼-in. pieces. Steak need not be partially frozen. Choice or corn-fed flank steak can be cooked like tender beef.

Microwave Stir-Fry

Microwave stir-fries taste like wok-fried, but you stir only 4 or 5 times, not constantly.

Beef & Pea Pods

Serve over rice or chow mein noodles with additional soy sauce, if desired.

Marinade:

¼ cup soy sauce
1 tablespoon cornstarch
2 tablespoons vegetable oil
1 slice fresh ginger root, minced or 1 teaspoon ground ginger
⅛ teaspoon garlic powder

Stir-fry:

1 lb. beef flank or sirloin steak, cut in ⅛ to ¼-in. strips, 1½ to 2-in. long
2 cups sliced mushrooms
1 pkg. (6-oz.) frozen pea pods defrosted in pkg. at High 1 to 2 min.

Serves 4

Pepper Steak Variation:

Omit mushrooms and pea pods and substitute 1 large green pepper, cut in ¼-in. strips, and 1 small onion, sliced and separated into rings.

How to Microwave Stir-Fry Beef & Pea Pods

Combine marinade ingredients in order given and stir in meat to coat well. Marinate at room temperature 20 to 30 minutes. Preheat 10-in. browning dish at High 5½ minutes.

Add meat and marinade quickly, stirring briskly until sizzling slows. Quickly add remaining ingredients; stir well.

Microwave at High 5½ to 8 minutes, or until vegetables are tender-crisp and meat is done, stirring every 2 minutes.

46

Lightly Barbecued Beef

1½ lbs. beef round steak, cut in
   ¼-in. strips
¼ cup flour
1 cup thinly sliced carrots
½ cup chopped onion
1 clove garlic, minced or
   pressed
¾ cup water
½ cup catsup
¼ cup brown sugar
2 tablespoons vinegar
1 tablespoon Worcestershire
   sauce
1 teaspoon salt
¼ teaspoon pepper

Serves 4 to 6

Toss beef and flour together in 3-qt. casserole. Add remaining ingredients; cover. Microwave at High 5 minutes.

Reduce power to 50% (Medium). Microwave 35 to 40 minutes, or until meat is tender, stirring after half the cooking time.

Let stand, covered, 10 minutes. Serve over rice or noodles.

Beef and Rice Pilaf

1 lb. beef round or chuck,
   cut into ¼-in. strips
2 cups instant or quick
   cooking rice
1¼ cups water
1 can (10¾-oz.) beef broth
1 medium onion, chopped
1 can (4-oz.) mushroom
   stems and pieces, drained
1 tablespoon parsley flakes
½ teaspoon salt
¼ teaspoon pepper
¼ teaspoon basil leaves
⅛ teaspoon garlic powder

Serves 4 to 6

Combine all ingredients in 3-qt. casserole. Cover tightly. Microwave at High 5 minutes.

Reduce power to 50% (Medium). Microwave 30 to 35 minutes, or until meat is tender and water is absorbed, stirring after half the cooking time.

Let stand, covered, 10 minutes.

Saucy Beef with Dumplings ▼

1½ lb. boneless beef round or
   chuck, cut in ¼-in. strips
¼ cup flour
2 stalks celery, thinly sliced
1 can (16-oz.) whole tomatoes
1 envelope dry onion soup mix
½ cup water

Dumplings:
2 cups biscuit mix
⅔ cup milk
1 tablespoon parsley flakes

Topping:
1 cup shredded cheddar
   cheese

Serves 4 to 6

Toss beef strips and flour together in a 3-qt. casserole. Add celery, tomatoes, soup mix and water. Cover tightly. Microwave at High 5 minutes.

Reduce power to 50% (Medium). Microwave 20 to 25 minutes, or until mixture thickens. Stir.

Combine biscuit mix, milk and parsley to make a soft dough. Drop by spoonfuls onto meat mixture. Microwave, uncovered, at 50% (Medium) 16 to 18 minutes, or until dumplings are set.

Sprinkle cheese over dumplings. Microwave at 50% (Medium) 3 to 4 minutes, or until cheese melts.

Beef Chunks

Cubed beef will be more tender if you cut it yourself from a chuck roast or steak. Supermarket stew meat is round, which is less marbled than chuck.

Texas Chili

1½ lb. chuck roast, cut into ½-in. cubes
1 medium onion, chopped
1 medium green pepper, chopped
1 clove garlic, minced or pressed
2 cans (16-oz.) kidney beans, drained
1 can (16-oz.) tomatoes, coarsely cut up
1 can (6-oz.) tomato paste
1 tablespoon brown sugar
1½ to 2 teaspoons chili powder
1 teaspoon parsley flakes
1 teaspoon salt
⅛ teaspoon pepper

Serves 4 to 6

Microwave at 50% (Medium) using times given below. To microwave at 30% (Low), increase cooking time to 1 hour, 25 minutes to 1 hour, 40 minutes.

How to Microwave Texas Chili

Combine all ingredients in 3-qt. casserole. Cover. Microwave at High 5 minutes.

Reduce power to 50% (Medium). Microwave 50 to 60 minutes, or until meat is fork tender, stirring after half the cooking time.

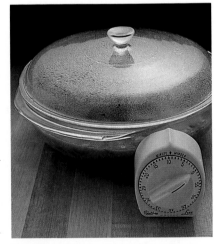

Let stand, covered, 10 minutes before serving.

Old-Fashioned Stew ▲

1¾ to 2 lb. stew meat or boneless chuck, ¾-in. cubes
⅓ cup flour
2 medium potatoes, peeled
   and cut into eighths
3 to 4 medium carrots, thinly
   sliced
1 stalk celery, cut in ¼-in.
   slices
1 large onion, sliced
1 clove garlic, minced or
   pressed
1 bay leaf
1 tablespoon instant beef
   bouillon
1 teaspoon sugar
1 teaspoon salt
¼ teaspoon pepper
1½ to 2 cups water
½ pkg. (10-oz.) frozen peas

Serves 4 to 6

Toss meat and flour together in
3-qt. casserole. Stir in remaining
ingredients except peas. Cover.
Microwave at High 5 minutes.
Reduce power to 50% (Medium).
Microwave 35 minutes.

Stir and re-cover. Microwave 40
to 45 minutes, or until meat is
fork tender, adding peas during
last 10 minutes. Let stand,
covered, 10 minutes.

To microwave at 30% (Low),
increase cooking times to 65
minutes and 65 to 75 minutes.

Stew for Two

¾ to 1 lb. stew meat or boneless chuck cut into ½ to
   ¾-in. cubes
2 tablespoons flour
1 medium potato, peeled and
   cut into ½ to ¾-in. cubes
1 cup thinly sliced carrots
1 medium onion, quartered
1 clove garlic, minced or
   pressed
1¼ cups water
½ cup red wine
1½ teaspoons instant beef
   bouillon
½ teaspoon salt
¼ teaspoon pepper
1 cup sliced fresh mushrooms

Serves 2 to 3

Toss meat and flour together in
3-qt. casserole. Large casserole
prevents boil over. Stir in
remaining ingredients except
mushrooms. Cover. Microwave
at High 3 minutes.

Reduce power to 50% (Medium).
Microwave 35 minutes. Stir in
mushrooms. Re-cover. Microwave 40 to 55 minutes, or until
meat is fork tender.

Let stand, covered, 10 minutes
before serving.

To microwave at 30% (Low),
increase cooking times to 60
minutes and 60 to 90 minutes.

Curried Beef Ragout

2 lb. beef round tip or boneless
   chuck, cut into ¾-in. cubes
¼ cup flour
2 large onions, sliced
¾ cup hot water
1 tablespoon instant beef
   bouillon
¾ cup red wine
1 tablespoon curry powder
½ teaspoon salt
¼ teaspoon pepper
1 cup dairy sour cream
1½ to 2 teaspoons creamed
   horseradish

Serves 6 to 8

Toss meat and flour together in
3-qt. casserole. Top with onion.
Dissolve bouillon in hot water.
Pour over meat. Mix in remaining ingredients except sour
cream and horseradish. Cover.
Microwave at High 5 minutes.

Reduce power to 50% (Medium).
Microwave 50 to 60 minutes, or
until meat is fork tender, stirring 2
or 3 times during cooking.

Let stand, covered, 10 minutes.
Blend in sour cream and
horseradish. Serve over noodles
or rice.

To microwave at 30% (Low),
increase cooking time to 1 hour,
25 minutes, to 1 hour, 40 minutes.

Beef & Cornbread Dinner in a Dish

1½ to 2 lb. beef round, cut in ½ to
   ¾-in. cubes
¼ cup flour
1 medium apple, chopped
½ cup onion, chopped
½ cup raisins
1 clove garlic, minced or
   pressed
1 cup water
1½ teaspoons curry (optional)

1 teaspoon salt
2 teaspoons instant beef
   bouillon
1 pkg. (10-oz.) cornbread mix
1 cup (4-oz.) shredded
   cheddar cheese
1 pkg. (10-oz.) frozen peas or
   peas and carrots, defrosted
   in box, 4 to 5 min. at High

Serves 6 to 8

Toss beef and flour together in 12×8-in. baking dish. Add apple, onion, raisins, garlic, water, seasonings and bouillon. Cover with plastic wrap. Microwave at High 5 minutes.

Reduce power to 50% (Medium). Microwave 40 to 50 minutes, or until meat is tender, stirring after half the cooking time.

Prepare cornbread and stir in cheese. Set aside. Top casserole with peas and carrots, then cornbread mixture. Microwave at High 6 to 9 minutes, or until cornbread is done, rotating dish halfway through cooking time. Let stand, covered with foil, 5 minutes.

Homemade Beef & Vegetable Soup

1½ lb. boneless beef chuck, cut
   into ½-in. cubes
3 medium carrots, cut into
   ¼-in. slices
2 medium potatoes, cut into
   ½-in. cubes
1 medium onion, sliced
1 cup shredded cabbage
1 can (16-oz.) stewed
   tomatoes

½ cup barley
1 quart water
1 tablespoon instant beef
   bouillon
1 tablespoon parsley flakes
1 bay leaf
1 teaspoon salt
¼ teaspoon pepper

Makes 4 quarts

Combine all ingredients in 5-qt. casserole. Cover. Microwave at High 10 minutes. Reduce power to 50% (Medium). Microwave 50 to 60 minutes, stirring after half the time, or until meat is tender and vegetables cooked. Let stand 10 minutes.

◄ Steak Kabobs

4 wooden skewers, 12-in. long
1 large green pepper, cut in
   24 ¾ to 1-in. cubes

1 pound beef tenderloin, cut in
   20 ¾ to 1-in. cubes
8 firm cherry tomatoes

Serves 4

On each skewer, alternate green pepper and beef cubes until there are 5 pieces of beef and 6 pieces of pepper on each skewer. Do not pack tightly.

Arrange kabobs on roasting rack. Microwave at High 6 to 9 minutes, until beef reaches desired doneness. (To test steak for doneness, see page 24.) Place a tomato on either end of skewer during last 2 minutes of cooking. Turn over and rearrange kabobs 2 or 3 times during microwaving.

Barbecued Beef Short Ribs

Short ribs are more tender and shrink less when they are cut in short lengths.

    3 to 3½ lb. beef short ribs, cut
        in 3-in. lengths
    ½ cup catsup
    ¼ cup chopped onion
    2 tablespoons lemon juice
    1 tablespoon butter or
        margarine, melted
    ½ small clove garlic, minced or
        pressed
    1½ teaspoons sugar
    ½ teaspoon salt
    ⅛ teaspoon pepper

                        Serves 4 to 6

Microwave at 50% (Medium) using times given below. To microwave at 30% (Low), increase cooking times to 35 minutes and 35 to 45 minutes.

How To Microwave Ribs

Place ribs in 12×8-in. dish. Combine catsup, onion, lemon juice and butter. Stir in seasonings. Pour half of sauce over ribs. Cover with vented plastic wrap. Microwave at High 5 minutes.

Reduce power to 50% (Medium). Microwave 20 minutes. Turn ribs over. If desired, drain and discard ½ to ¾ cup of liquid. Pour remaining sauce over ribs.

Re-cover. Microwave 20 to 25 minutes, or until ribs are fork tender. Let stand, covered, 5 to 10 minutes before serving.

Ground Beef

Traditional Meatloaf

1½ lb. ground beef
1 egg
¼ cup finely crushed round
  buttery crackers
1 small onion, chopped
¼ cup finely chopped celery

1 tablespoon catsup
1 tablespoon Worcestershire
  sauce
1 teaspoon salt
¼ teaspoon pepper

Serves 4 to 6

How to Microwave Traditional Meatloaf

Combine all ingredients well. Spread mixture in dish evenly. Do not cover.

Microwave loaf at High 13 to 18 minutes, rotating dish ½ turn after half the cooking time.

Test center of loaf. Meat should be firm and have lost its pink color. Let stand, uncovered, 5 minutes. (145° to 155°)

◄ Savory Rolled Meatloaf

Meatloaf:
1½ lb. ground beef
2 eggs
¼ cup dry bread crumbs
1 tablespoon Worcestershire
  sauce
1 teaspoon salt

Filling:
1 cup chopped green pepper
¾ cup chopped onion
1 jar (2-oz.) diced pimiento,
  drained

Serves 4 to 6

Mix meatloaf ingredients together well. On wax paper, pat into a rectangle ½-in. thick.

Microwave green pepper at High 1½ minutes or until slightly softened (for soft peppers, Microwave 30 to 40 seconds longer). Sprinkle green pepper, onion and pimiento over meat, leaving 1-in. borders on all sides. Roll up as shown at right, pressing edges together to seal. Place in loaf dish, seam side down. Microwave at High 5 minutes.

Reduce power to 50% (Medium). Microwave 20 to 30 minutes, or until meat loses its pink color (internal temperature 145° to 150°), rotating dish ½ turn halfway through the cooking time. Let stand 5 minutes before serving.

Roll meatloaf by starting on short side. Lift paper until meat begins to roll tightly. Peel back paper to keep it free. Continue to lift and peel until complete.

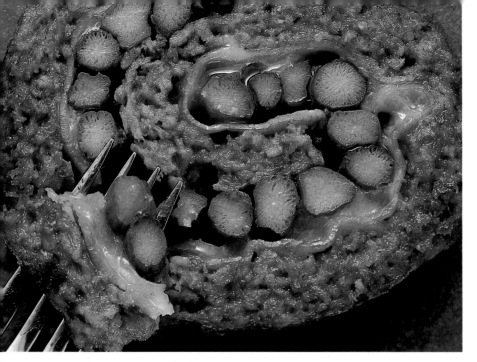

Ham, Cheese and ▲ Asparagus Loaf

Meatloaf:
1½ lb. ground beef
 2 eggs
 ¼ cup dry bread crumbs
 2 tablespoons milk
 1 teaspoon seasoned salt

Filling:
 3 slices boiled ham
 3 slices Mozzarella cheese
 1 pkg. (10-oz.) frozen
  asparagus spears

Serves 6 to 8

Microwave asparagus in its package at High 5 minutes. Meanwhile, mix meatloaf ingredients together well. On wax paper, pat into a 9×13-in. rectangle, ½-in. thick.

Top meat with ham slices; follow with cheese and asparagus, leaving a 1-in. border on all sides. Roll up as shown on page 53. Place in loaf dish, seam side down. Microwave at High 5 minutes.

Reduce power to 50% (Medium). Microwave 20 to 30 minutes, rotating dish ½ turn halfway through cooking time, until meat is firm and has lost its pink color (internal temperature 145° to 150°). Let stand 5 minutes before serving.

Curried Meatloaf

Meatloaf:
1½ lb. ground beef
 ¼ cup quick cooking oats
 2 eggs
 1 teaspoon salt
 ¼ teaspoon pepper
1½ teaspoons curry powder
 1 small onion, chopped
 ½ cup celery, chopped
 1 apple, peeled, grated and
  divided
 ½ cup raisins

Sauce:
 ¼ cup catsup
 2 tablespoons brown sugar
 ¼ teaspoon curry powder

Serves 4 to 6

Mix together all meatloaf ingredients except raisins, using only half the apple. Press half the meat mixture into loaf dish. Sprinkle with raisins and remaining apple, leaving 1-in. borders on all sides. Top with remaining meat mixture, pressing edges together to seal. Microwave at High 13 to 18 minutes. Drain.

Combine sauce ingredients. Pour over meatloaf. Microwave at High 2 to 3 minutes, until meat is set (internal temperature 145° to 150°). Let stand 5 minutes before serving.

Ricotta Meat Roll

This attractive loaf is rich in protein and can be made as low-calorie as you wish. Smooth ricotta has a higher fat content than cottage cheese, but is available made with part-skim milk. If you use cottage cheese, beat or blend it until smooth.

Meatloaf:
1½ lb. ground beef
 2 eggs
 ¼ cup chopped onion
 ¼ cup dry bread crumbs
 1 tablespoon Worcestershire
  sauce
 1 teaspoon salt

Filling:
 ½ cup ricotta or cottage
  cheese
 ¼ cup dry bread crumbs
 1 egg
 ¼ cup sliced almonds
 1 can (8-oz.) cut green beans,
  drained
 ⅛ to ¼ teaspoon thyme,
  crushed
 ⅛ teaspoon basil, crushed

Serves 4 to 6

Mix meatloaf ingredients together well. On wax paper, pat into a rectangle ½-in. thick.

Combine filling ingredients. Spread over meat, leaving 1-in. borders on all sides. Roll up as shown on page 53. Press edges of meat together to seal. Place in loaf dish, seam side down. Microwave at High 5 minutes.

Reduce power to 50% (Medium). Microwave 20 to 30 minutes, rotating dish ½ turn halfway through the cooking time, until meat is firm and loses its pink color (internal temperature 145° to 150°). Let stand 5 minutes before serving.

Six-Layer Meatloaf Ring

Meatloaf:

1½ lb. ground beef
2 eggs
½ medium onion, chopped
¼ cup dry bread crumbs
1 tablespoon Worcestershire sauce
1 teaspoon seasoned salt

Filling:

¾ cup water
2 tablespoons butter
¼ teaspoon thyme (optional)
2 cups dry seasoned stuffing mix

Topping:

1 can (4-oz.) sliced mushrooms, drained, divided
½ medium onion, sliced and separated into rings

Serves 4 to 6

Combine loaf ingredients and mix well. Divide into thirds. Measure water into a 1-qt. measure. Add butter and thyme; microwave at High 1¼ to 1¾ minutes until boiling. Stir in stuffing mix. Assemble loaf as shown below.

Microwave at High 5 minutes. Reduce power to 50% (Medium). Microwave 8 to 13 minutes, rotating dish ½ turn halfway through cooking time, until meat is firm and has lost its pink color. Turn out on platter to serve.

How to Layer Meatloaf

Place half the mushrooms in bottom of ring mold. Top with onion rings. Cover with ⅓ loaf mixture.

Mix remaining mushrooms into stuffing. Spoon half of stuffing over meat in ring, leaving 1-in. borders. Top with second ⅓ of meat mixture.

Press edges firmly to seal. Repeat with remaining stuffing and meat. Seal edges.

Bacon Cheeseburgers

Microwave bacon on a roasting rack (page 94), allowing 1 or 2 slices per burger. Set aside on paper towel. Microwave patties on rack. After cooking, place bacon slices on each patty and top with a slice of cheese. Cheese melts during standing time. If necessary, return patty to oven for 15 seconds to 1 minute, watching through the oven door, until cheese is as soft as desired.

The charts below are for medium done, ¼-lb. hamburgers, ½-in. thick. If you prefer well done or medium rare, add or subtract ½ minute of cooking time.

Browning Dish

High Power

Quantity	1st side Minutes	2nd side Minutes
2	1¼	¾-1½
4	2	1½-2¾
6	2½	2½-3¼

Plate or Rack

High Power

Quantity	1st side Minutes	2nd side Minutes
2	1½	1-1½
4	2	1½-2½
6	3	3-3½

Browning Dish Burgers

Preheat dish according to manufacturers' directions. Place patties in browning dish. Microwave first side. Turn over. Rearrange patties if cooking more than four. Microwave second side.

Roasting Rack or Plate Burgers

Place patties on a roasting rack or plate lined with paper towels. Brush with equal parts bouquet sauce and water, if desired. Cover with wax paper. Microwave first side. Turn over, rearranging patties if you are cooking more than four. Brush with sauce mixture. Cover. Microwave second side. Let stand 1 to 2 minutes.

Salisbury Steak

1 lb. ground beef
1 egg
¼ cup dry bread crumbs
1 tablespoon Worcestershire
    sauce
1 teaspoon seasoned salt
1 medium carrot, grated
¼ cup diced onion
¼ cup diced celery
¼ cup diced green pepper
1 envelope onion gravy mix
¾ cup water
    Toasted English muffins

Serves 4

Mix ground beef, egg, bread crumbs and Worcestershire sauce together well. Add salt and vegetables. Shape into 4 patties. Place in 8×8-in. dish. If desired, brush with a mixture of equal amounts of bouquet sauce and water. Cover with wax paper. Microwave at High 4 minutes.

Turn patties over; brush again with sauce. Cover and microwave 2½ to 4½ minutes. Drain. Cover and let stand while preparing gravy.

Combine gravy mix and water in 1-qt. container. Microwave at High 3 to 5 minutes, or until sauce is thick and smooth, stirring every minute.

To serve, place patties on toasted English muffins and top with sauce.

Stuffed Burgers

1 lb. ground beef
2 tablespoons shredded cheese

Serves 4

Shape ground beef into 8 patties, 4-in. in diameter. Place shredded cheese in the center of 4 patties. Top with remaining patties and press edges together to seal.

Roasting Rack High Power Patties, 4-in. diameter		
Quantity	1st side Minutes	2nd side Minutes
2	2	2-3
4	3	3½-4½
6	4	4½-5½

Burgers with Wild Rice

1 lb. ground beef
1 egg
1 teaspoon seasoned salt
1 can (4-oz.) sliced mushrooms,
    drained

1 pkg. (6½-oz.) quick cooking
    wild rice mix
    Butter or margarine
    Water

Serves 4

Mix ground beef, egg and salt together well. Shape into 4 burgers.

In a 2-qt. casserole, combine mushrooms with contents of rice mix, butter or margarine and water as package directs, using ½ cup less liquid than called for. Top rice with burgers. cover with plastic wrap. Microwave at High 5 minutes.

Reduce power to 50% (Medium). Microwave 3 to 5 minutes or until rice has absorbed most of the water.

Uncover. Brush burgers with a mixture of equal parts bouquet sauce and water. Microwave at High 3 to 5 minutes or until casserole is desired consistency.

Variations: Use one or more of the following to make a total of 2 tablespoons stuffing per burger.

Crumbled cooked bacon
Chopped ripe or stuffed olives
Chopped onion
Chopped green pepper
Chopped water chestnuts
Chopped mushrooms

Browning Dish High Power Patties, 4-in. diameter		
Quantity	1st side Minutes	2nd side Minutes
2	1	1-2
4	1¼	2-3¾
6	1½	4½-5½

Basic Meatballs

1 lb. ground beef	1 teaspoon salt
1 egg	½ teaspoon dry mustard
¼ cup chopped onion	¼ teaspoon oregano leaves
¼ cup fine dry bread crumbs	⅛ teaspoon pepper

Combine all ingredients. Shape into 12 large or 20 small meatballs.

High Power	
Large Meatballs 7-9 min.	Small Meatballs 8-10 min.

How to Microwave Basic Meatballs

Arrange meatballs in 10-in. pie plate or 12×8-in. dish. Microwave at High 4 to 5 minutes.

Rotate large meatballs or rearrange small ones. Microwave remaining time. Serve with gravy, if desired.

How to Microwave Meatballs with Sauce

Arrange meatballs in dish with space between them, if possible. Add sauce as directed in recipes and microwave at High.

Turn over and rearrange meatballs once or twice during microwaving. Make sure those in the center of dish are brought to the outside.

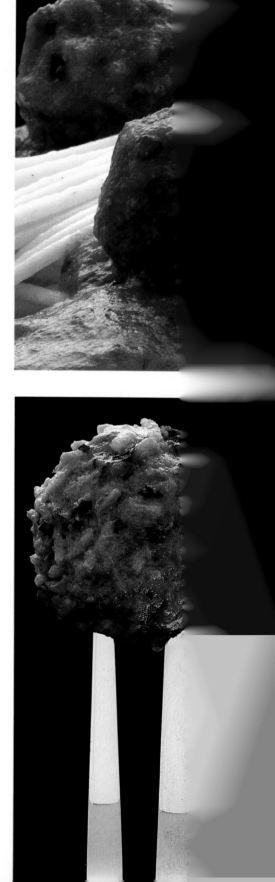

◄ Porcupine Meatballs

1 lb. ground beef
1 cup instant or quick
   cooking rice
1 can (16-oz.) tomato sauce,
   divided
1 egg
1 teaspoon onion powder
½ teaspoon salt
¼ teaspoon pepper
1½ teaspoons parsley flakes
½ teaspoon dry mustard

Serves 4

Mix ground beef, rice, ½ cup tomato sauce, egg, onion powder, salt and pepper together well. Shape into 12 meatballs. Place in 12×8-in. dish.

Combine remaining tomato sauce, parsley flakes and mustard. Pour over meatballs. Cover with wax paper. Microwave at High 4 minutes.

Rearrange meatballs. Cover. Microwave at High 4 to 6 minutes, or until meat is firm.

Italian Meatballs ▲

Meatballs:
1 lb. ground beef
1 egg
¼ cup chopped onion
¼ cup chopped green pepper
¼ cup grated Parmesan cheese

Sauce:
1 can (16-oz.) tomato sauce
1 teaspoon parsley flakes
¼ teaspoon basil leaves
¼ teaspoon oregano leaves
⅛ teaspoon garlic powder

Serves 4 to 6

Mix meatball ingredients together. Shape into 20 meatballs. Place in a 2-qt. casserole. Microwave at High 5 to 7 minutes or until meatballs are set. Rotate dish and rearrange the meatballs once or twice during cooking.

Combine sauce ingredients; pour over meatballs. Microwave at High 5½ to 9½ minutes or until heated through, stirring once during cooking. Serve over spaghetti.

Pizza Meatball Variation:
Reduce tomato sauce to one 8-oz. can. Add 1 can (6-oz.) tomato paste and ½ cup chopped stuffed olives. After sauce has been poured over meatballs microwave 4½ to 6½ minutes. Top with 1 cup shredded Mozzarella cheese. Microwave at 50% (Medium) 2 to 4 minutes, or until cheese melts.

Stuffed Meat Cups ▲

Meat Cups:
1 lb. ground beef
1 egg
¼ cup dry bread crumbs
2 tablespoons catsup
½ teaspoon salt
¼ teaspoon pepper

Filling:
1 can (4-oz.) sliced
   mushrooms, drained
1 cup shredded cheddar
   cheese
½ cup sliced green onion

Serves 4

Mix all meat cup ingredients together well. Divide ⅔ of this mixture into 4 equal portions and press into 4 custard cups to form a crust or shell.

Combine filling ingredients. Place equal amounts in each meat cup. Shape remaining meat mixture into 4 patties. Place over filling and press meat edges together to seal.

Place paper toweling beneath cups to catch possible drippings. Microwave at High 8 to 10 minutes, rotating and rearranging cups after half the cooking time, or until meat is firm and most of red color is gone. Cover with foil; let stand 5 minutes before serving.

Filling Variation 1:
1 pkg. (10-oz.) frozen
   chopped spinach or
   broccoli, defrosted* and
   drained thoroughly
1 cup shredded Swiss cheese
4 slices bacon, cooked and
   crumbled

Filling Variation 2:
1 can (4-oz.) sliced
   mushrooms, drained
1 pkg. (2-oz.) cream cheese,
   softened
¼ cup crumbled blue cheese
¼ cup dry bread crumbs

*Microwave in package at High 3 to 4 minutes.

Stuffed Green Peppers

4 large green peppers
1 lb. ground beef
½ cup chopped onion
¼ cup chopped celery
1 can (6-oz.) tomato paste
1 cup cooked rice
1 teaspoon seasoned salt
1 clove garlic, minced

Serves 4

Cut tops off the peppers; chop tops and set aside. Core and seed peppers. Place cut side up in 8×8-in. dish.

Crumble ground beef into 2-qt. casserole; add onion, celery and chopped pepper tops. Microwave at High 4 to 6 minutes or until meat is cooked and vegetables are tender. Stir to break up meat; drain. Add remaining ingredients and mix together well.

Fill peppers with stuffing mixture. Cover dish with plastic wrap. Microwave at High 8 to 11 minutes, or until peppers are tender-crisp; rotating dish after half the cooking time.

Cabbage Rolls

To remove cabbage leaves, microwave the whole cabbage head 1½ to 3½ minutes, until 8 outer leaves can be easily separated. Refrigerate remaining cabbage for future use.

8 large cabbage leaves

Filling:
 1 lb. ground beef
¼ cup chopped onion
 1 cup cooked rice
 1 teaspoon salt
 1 egg

Sauce:
 1 can (16 oz.) tomato sauce
 1 tablespoon brown sugar
½ teaspoon basil leaves
½ teaspoon oregano leaves

Serves 4

Shape cabbage rolls as shown below.

Combine sauce ingredients and pour over rolls. Cover with wax paper. Microwave at High 8 minutes. Baste rolls with sauce, rotate dish ½ turn and re-cover. Microwave 6½ to 8½ minutes, or until meat is set.

How to Shape Cabbage Rolls

Cut out hard center rib from each cabbage leaf. Place leaves in an 8×12-in. baking dish. Cover with vented plastic wrap. Microwave at High 1½ to 3 minutes, or until leaves are pliable. Set aside.

Combine filling ingredients well. Shape mixture into 8 small loaves. Overlap cut edges of cabbage leaves and place a loaf on the base of each leaf.

Fold in sides of leaves. Roll up leaves to enclose filling. Place rolls, seam side down, around sides of an 8×12-in. dish, keeping center empty.

Mexican Casserole

4 to 5 frozen flour tortillas
1 lb. ground beef
½ cup chopped green pepper
½ cup chopped onion
1 envelope (1¼-oz.) taco
    seasoning mix
1 can (8-oz.) tomato sauce
1 can (6-oz.) tomato paste
½ cup sliced pitted ripe olives
¼ cup water
½ teaspoon chili powder
1 cup dairy sour cream
2 eggs
¼ teaspoon pepper
2 cups broken corn chips
2 cups shredded Monterey
    Jack cheese

Serves 4 to 6

Photo directions opposite.

Hamburger Stroganoff

1 lb. ground beef
1 can (10¾-oz.) cream of
    mushroom soup
1 can (4-oz.) sliced
    mushrooms, drained
½ cup sliced green onion
¼ cup catsup
½ teaspoon dry mustard
½ teaspoon salt
1 cup dairy sour cream

Serves 4 to 6

Crumble ground beef into 2-qt. casserole. Cover. Microwave at High 4 to 5 minutes or until meat loses pink color, stirring halfway through cooking time. Do not drain.

Add all remaining ingredients except sour cream; mix well. Cover. Microwave at High 4 to 6 minutes or until heated through. Stir after 3 minutes.

Blend in sour cream. Microwave at High 1½ to 3 minutes or until hot. Stir once. Serve over rice or noodles.

How to Microwave Mexican Casserole

Place frozen tortillas between paper towels. Microwave at High 30 to 60 seconds. Separate. Crumble ground beef into a 2-qt. casserole.

Add green pepper and onions. Microwave at High 3 to 5 minutes or until meat loses its pink color and vegetables are tender-crisp. Stir and drain.

Mix in taco seasoning, tomato sauce and paste, olives, water and chili powder. Microwave at 50% (Medium) 10 to 15 minutes, or until thickened.

Blend sour cream, eggs and pepper together in a small bowl. Place 2 tortillas on bottom of 12×8-in. dish.

Top with half the meat mixture followed by half the sour cream mixture. Repeat layers with remaining ingredients.

Sprinkle with corn chips and cheese. Microwave at 50% 10 to 15 minutes or until cheese melts. Let stand 5 minutes.

Hamburger, Spinach and Noodle Casserole

1 pkg. (10-oz.) frozen
   chopped spinach
1 lb. ground beef
1 can (4-oz.) mushroom
   pieces and stems,
   drained
1 can (10¾-oz.) cream of
   mushroom soup

½ cup ricotta cheese
½ teaspoon salt
¼ teaspoon pepper
1½ cups cooked medium egg
   noodles
1 can (3-oz.) French fried
   onions, divided

Serves 4 to 6

Microwave spinach in its box, at High 3 to 4 minutes. Break into small pieces; drain well. Crumble ground beef into 2-qt. casserole. Microwave at High 3 to 5 minutes, until meat loses its pink color. Stir to break up meat; drain.

Combine spinach, mushrooms, soup, cheese and seasonings with hamburger. Add noodles and half of onions. Microwave at High 5 minutes. Stir. Sprinkle with remaining onions. Microwave at High 5 to 7 minutes or until heated through.

Hamburger Pie ▲

Crust:
  1 lb. ground beef
  1 egg
  ¼ cup dry bread crumbs
  1 tablespoon soy sauce
  1 teaspoon dry mustard
  ¼ teaspoon ground cumin
  ⅛ teaspoon garlic powder

Filling:
1½ cups sliced potatoes (⅛-in.
  thick)

¾ cup sliced onion,
  separated into rings
1 cup sliced mushrooms

Topping:
  1 cup shredded cheddar
  cheese
  ½ cup shredded Swiss
  cheese
1½ teaspoons parsley flakes

Serves 4 to 6

Combine all crust ingredients and mix well. Press into 9-in. pie pan. Microwave at High 3 to 5 minutes or until meat is set (some pink may remain), rotating once or twice during cooking. Drain.

Top the meat with a layer of potato slices; follow with onions, and then mushrooms. Cover with plastic wrap. Microwave at High 4½ to 8½ minutes or until potatoes in center are fork tender, rotating once during cooking.

Reduce power to 50% (Medium). Sprinkle with cheeses and parsley. Microwave, uncovered, 2 to 5 minutes or until cheese melts. Let stand 2 to 3 minutes before serving.

Ground Beef Hash

  1 lb. ground beef
  3 medium potatoes, peeled
  and cut in ¼-in. cubes,
  (3 cups)
⅓ cup catsup
⅔ cup water
  1 envelope dry onion soup mix

Serves 4 to 6

Crumble ground beef into 2-qt. casserole. Microwave at High 3 to 5 minutes or until meat is cooked. Stir to break up meat; drain.

Mix in remaining ingredients and cover with tight-fitting lid or plastic wrap. Microwave at High 12 to 15 minutes or until potatoes are tender, stirring after half the cooking time.

Sloppy Joes

1 lb. ground beef
1 medium onion, chopped
1 can (10¾-oz.) chicken
   gumbo soup
½ cup catsup
¼ cup brown sugar
1 tablespoon vinegar
2 teaspoons mustard
½ teaspoon salt

Serves 4 to 6

Crumble ground beef into 2-qt. casserole; add onion. Microwave at High 4 to 6 minutes or until meat is cooked and onion is tender. Stir to break up meat; drain.

Mix in remaining ingredients. Microwave at High 5 to 7 minutes or until heated thoroughly, stirring once during cooking.

Hamburger Bean Pot

4 slices bacon, cut in eighths
1 lb. ground beef
1 medium onion, chopped
   (½ cup)
1 medium apple, peeled and
   diced (1 cup)
1 can (16-oz.) pork and beans
   in tomato sauce
¼ cup molasses
¼ cup barbecue sauce
1 cup broken corn chips

Serves 4 to 6

Place bacon in 2-qt. casserole. Cover with paper towel. Microwave at High 4½ to 6½ minutes or until crisp. Add crumbled ground beef, onion and apple. Microwave at High 4 to 6 minutes. Stir to break up meat; drain.

Add all remaining ingredients except corn chips. Microwave at High 7 to 9 minutes or until hot and bubbly, stirring after half the cooking time. Top with chips before serving.

Beef Leftovers

A microwave oven reheats food without a "leftover" flavor. Casseroles containing cubed beef are heated at 50% (Medium) to keep beef tender.

Barbecued Beef Strips

  1 medium onion, finely chopped
  2 cups cooked beef cut into thin, wide strips
  1 can (8-oz.) tomato sauce
  ½ cup catsup
  ¼ cup brown sugar
  1 tablespoon Worcestershire sauce
  ½ teaspoon dry mustard
  ½ teaspoon chili powder
  ½ tespoon salt
  ⅛ teaspoon pepper

Serves 4 to 6

Combine all ingredients well in a 1½-qt. casserole. Microwave at High 10 to 12 minutes, or until hot and bubbly, stirring 2 to 3 times during cooking. Serve in hamburger buns.

Quick Beef Casserole

  1 can (10¾-oz.) cream of mushroom soup
  1 can (10½-oz.) chicken with rice soup
  2 cups cubed cooked beef
  1 small onion, finely chopped
  1 clove garlic, minced or pressed
  1 can (3-oz.) chow mein noodles, divided
  ½ cup sliced almonds

Serves 4 to 6

Blend soups together in 2-qt. casserole. Mix in beef, onion, garlic and all but ¾ cup chow mein noodles. Cover. Microwave at High 3 minutes.

Reduce power to 50% (Medium). Microwave 5 to 7 minutes.

Stir. Sprinkle with almonds and remaining chow mein noodles. Microwave 5 minutes, uncovered, or until heated through.

66

Speedy Beef Chow Mein

1 medium onion, sliced and
  separated into rings
½ medium green pepper, cut
  into ½-in. strips
1 tablespoon butter or margarine
¾ cup water
2 tablespoons soy sauce
2 tablespoons cornstarch
1 tablespoon brown sugar

1 teaspoon instant beef bouillon
¼ teaspoon ground ginger
2 cups cooked beef cut into thin
  strips
1 can (16-oz.) chow mein
  vegetables, rinsed and
  drained
1 can (4-oz.) mushroom stems
  and pieces, drained

Serves 4 to 6

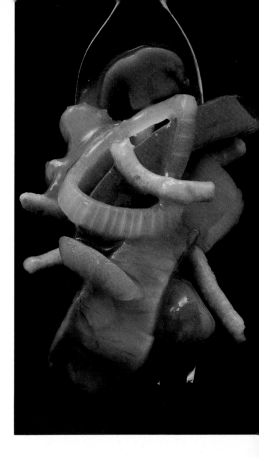

Combine onion, green pepper and butter in 2-qt. casserole. Cover. Microwave at High 2 to 3 minutes or until vegetables are tender-crisp. Set aside.

In a 2-cup measure, stir water, soy sauce, cornstarch, and brown sugar together until smooth. Add bouillon. Microwave at High 3 to 4 minutes, or until thickened, stirring 1 or 2 times during cooking.

Mix sauce and remaining ingredients with cooked vegetables. Microwave at High 4 to 6 minutes, stirring 1 or 2 times, until heated through.

Serve over rice, noodles or chow mein noodles.

Hot Beef Sandwich

1 serving instant mashed
  potatoes, using proportions
  given on pkg.
1 slice toast

1 slice leftover roast beef,
  ¼-in. thick, or enough for a
  thin layer
4 to 6 tablespoons canned or
  leftover beef gravy

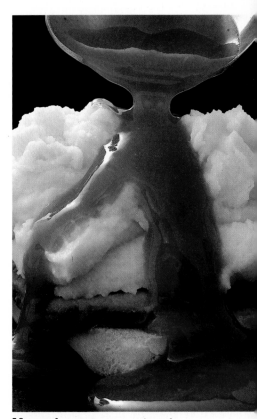

How to Microwave a Hot Beef Sandwich

Combine in a 2-cup measure, water, butter and salt for potatoes. Microwave at High ¾ to 1½ minutes, or until water boils. Blend in milk and potato flakes.

Place 1 slice toast on plate. Top with large slice of leftover roast beef.

Mound potatoes on beef. Spoon gravy over potatoes. Microwave at High ¾ to 1¼ minutes, or until heated through.

Veal

Veal is naturally fine-grained and tender, but it has little or no marbling. It should be shielded with strips of fat, coated with sauce or crumbs, or microwaved covered to keep it moist. Microwaved veal responds well to seasonings, and is complemented by a flavorful sauce.

Milk-fed baby veal, which has pale pink lean flesh, is hard to obtain unless you live near a foreign specialty market. Most veal sold in the United States is calf, which has been fed on grass or grain.

Color is the best gauge of age and tenderness. Older calves have deep pink to light red flesh. Good veal of any age should have firm, white exterior fat and porous bones.

Store veal as directed for beef, page 16. While chops and cutlets stay fresh several days, their flavor is most delicate when they are cooked within 24 hours.

◄ Veal Parmesan, page 72.

Veal Storage Chart

Cut	Refrigerator	Freezer Compartment	Freezer +0° or below
Roasts	3-4 days	No more than 1 week unless you are sure temperature is below 0° Defrosting times are based on 0° freezer temperature.	3-4 months
Chops & Cutlets	1-3 days		3-4 months
Stuffed Breast or Chops	24 hours		3-4 months
Ground Veal	24 hours		3-4 months

Veal Defrosting Chart

Cut	Comments	50% (Medium)	30% (Low)
Roasts	Follow directions for roasts over 2-in. thick, page 20, but let veal stand 20 minutes after half the defrosting time, and 20 to 30 minutes after defrosting.	8½-11½ min. per lb.	14¼-18¾ min. per lb.
Chops & Cutlets	Follow directions for small steaks, page 21, but let stand 10 to 15 minutes after defrosting.	4-6 min. per lb.	6½-10 min. per lb.
Ground Veal	Follow directions for ground beef, page 22. Scrape frequently to remove defrosted pieces.	3¾-4¾ min. per lb.	5-7 min. per lb.

Veal Roasts

Veal is always roasted well done, but it dries out easily because it contains little fat. Use a microwave thermometer or probe; remove the roast from the oven at 160° and let it stand to complete cooking to 165° to 170°. Orange Marmalade helps seal in juices. For variety, substitute sage for rosemary and currant jelly for the marmalade.

The most common veal roasts are from the leg and shoulder. A shoulder roast should be boned and rolled; the shoulder blade roast is uneven in shape and has a complicated bone structure which makes it difficult to carve.

Chart at right shows popular retail cuts of veal and the wholesale cuts from which they are taken. It was adapted for microwaving from information supplied by the National Livestock and Meat Board.

Approx. Time	Start at High	Finish at 50%
13½-17½ min. per lb.	First 5 min.	160°

How to Insert Probe or Thermometer in a Veal Roast

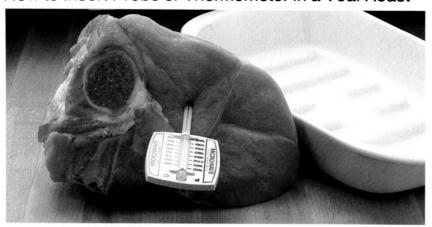

Rump or Round Roast. Insert sensor into largest muscle, parallel to the bone, so tip is in center of meatiest area.

Rolled Roasts. Insert sensor from end or side so tip is in center of roast.

How to Microwave Veal Roasts

Rub roast with rosemary. Place roast, fat side down, on rack in baking dish. Coat with ½ jar (10-oz.) orange marmalade. Insert thermometer, if used, so tip is in center of meat, not touching bone.

Estimate the total cooking time; divide in half. Microwave at High 5 minutes. Reduce power to 50% (Medium). Microwave remaining part of first half of time. Turn roast over.

Coat with remaining marmalade. Insert probe, if used. Microwave until roast reaches internal temperature of 160°. Let stand 10 minutes, tented with foil. Temperature will rise to 165° to 170°.

SHOULDER

3 Arm Roast (Shoulder or Round Bone) Microwave covered or uncovered.

Blade Roast (Shoulder) Microwave covered or uncovered. **2**

2,3 Boneless Shoulder Roast (Rolled Shoulder) Microwave covered or uncovered.

Arm Steak 3 (Shoulder steak, Round Bone steak or chop) Microwave covered or sauced.

2 Blade Steak (Shoulder steak or chop) Microwave covered or uncovered.

Veal for Stew 1,2,3

(Large pieces)   (Small pieces)
Microwave covered.

RIB

4

Rib Roast Microwave uncovered.

Crown 4 Roast Microwave uncovered.

Rib Chop 4 Microwave covered or sauced.

Boneless 4 Rib Chop Microwave covered or sauced.

LOIN

1

Loin Roast Microwave uncovered.

Kidney Chop 1 Microwave covered or sauced.

Loin Chop 1 Microwave covered or sauced.

Top Loin Chop 1 Microwave covered or sauced.

SIRLOIN

1

Sirloin Roast Microwave uncovered.

Boneless 1 Sirloin Roast (Rolled Double Sirloin) Microwave uncovered.

Sirloin Steak 1 (Sirloin chop) Microwave covered or sauced.

Cubed Steak Microwave covered or sauced.

ROUND
Leg

2 Rump Roast Microwave covered or uncovered.

Round 3,4 Roast Microwave covered or uncovered.

2 Boneless Rump Roast Microwave covered or uncovered.

Round 3,4 Steak Microwave covered or sauced.

Cutlets 1,3,4 Microwave covered or sauced.

Cutlets (Thin slices) Microwave covered or sauced.

Rolled Cutlets Microwave covered or sauced. **1,3,4**

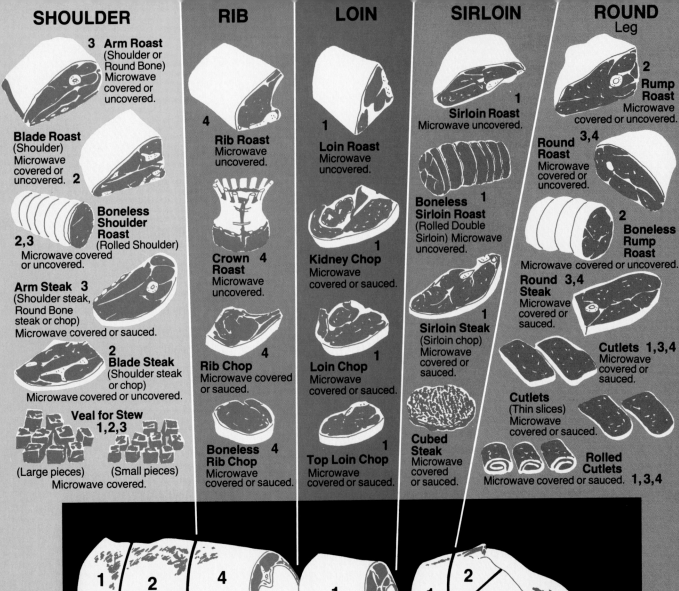

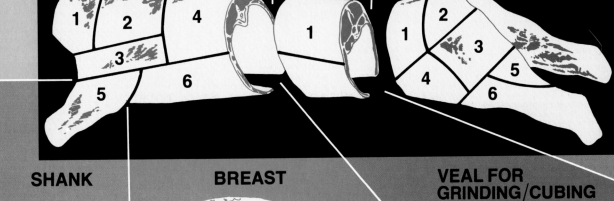

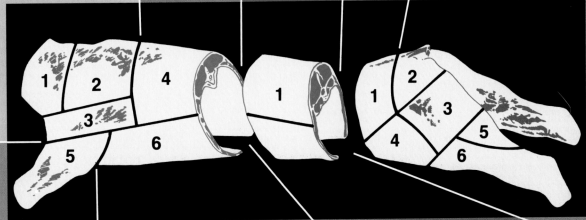

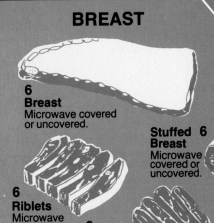

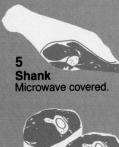

SHANK

5 Shank Microwave covered.

5 Shank Cross Cuts Microwave covered.

BREAST

6 Breast Microwave covered or uncovered.

Stuffed 6 Breast Microwave covered or uncovered.

6 Riblets Microwave covered.

6 Boneless Riblets Microwave covered.

6 Stuffed Chops Microwave covered or sauced.

VEAL FOR GRINDING/CUBING

Veal Cubes for Kabobs (City Chicken) Microwave covered or sauced.

Mock Chicken Legs Microwave covered or sauced.

Veal Cutlets

These thin slices have no muscle separations or bone. They can be made from veal round steak.

Veal in Sour Cream Sauce

4 veal cutlets, 1-lb., flattened to ¼-in. thickness
¼ to ½ cup flour
1 tablespoon butter or margarine, melted
1 tablespoon olive or vegetable oil
1 cup dairy sour cream
¼ cup dry vermouth
2 tablespoons water
1 teaspoon flour
½ teaspoon salt
⅛ teaspoon pepper

Serves 4

Dredge cutlets in flour. Preheat 10-in. browning dish at High 5 minutes. Add butter, oil and cutlets. Microwave 1 minute on each side.

In 2-cup measure, combine remaining ingredients until smooth. Pour over cutlets. Cover. Reduce power to 50% (Medium). Microwave 7 to 10 minutes, or until cutlets are tender, turning cutlets over and stirring sauce after half the cooking time.

How to Flatten Veal Cutlets

Pound cutlet with bottom of small heavy skillet or flat side of meat mallet. Serrated side of mallet tears meat.

Hungarian Veal Paprika

1 pkg. (6¼-oz.) noodles with sour cream and cheese sauce mix
2 cups hot water
2 tablespoons butter or margarine
2 tablespoons flour
½ teaspoon salt
⅛ teaspoon pepper
4 veal cutlets, 1-lb., flattened to ¼-in. thickness
Paprika

Serves 4

In 12×8-in. baking dish, combine noodles, sauce mix, water and butter. Stir to dissolve sauce mix. Cover with plastic wrap. Microwave at High 5 minutes. Reduce power to 50% (Medium). Microwave 10 to 12 minutes, or until noodles are tender. Stir.

Combine flour, salt and pepper. Dredge cutlets in flour mixture; place them on top of noodles. Cover with wax paper.

Microwave 8 to 10 minutes, or until veal is tender. Turn cutlets over. Sprinkle casserole generously with paprika. Microwave, uncovered, 3 to 5 minutes. Garnish with parsley, if desired.

Veal Parmesan

Sauce:
¼ cup chopped onion, optional
1 can (8-oz.) tomato sauce
½ teaspoon salt
⅛ teaspoon pepper
⅛ teaspoon oregano

Coating:
⅓ cup grated Parmesan cheese

Veal & Dumplings ▶

Veal:
1 cup flour
1 teaspoon paprika
½ teaspoon salt
¼ teaspoon thyme
⅛ teaspoon pepper
4 veal cutlets, 1-1½ lbs. total, flattened to ¼-in. thickness
2 tablespoons butter or margaine
2 medium onions, cut in quarters
1 can (10¾-oz.) cream of chicken soup
1 can (4-oz.) mushroom stems and pieces, undrained

Dumplings:
1 cup flour
2 teaspoons baking powder
2 teaspoons poppy seed
1 teaspoon dried chives
¼ teaspoon salt
¼ teaspoon thyme
¼ cup milk
1 egg
2 tablespoons butter or margarine, melted
¼ to ⅓ cup seasoned bread crumbs

Serves 4

2 tablespoons corn flakes or dry bread crumbs
4 veal cutlets, 1-1½ lbs., flattened to ¼-in. thickness

1 egg, slightly beaten
1 cup (4-oz.) shredded mozarella cheese
Grated Parmesan cheese

Serves 4

In 2-cup measure, combine sauce ingredients. Microwave at High 2 minutes. Reduce power to 50% (Medium). Microwave 5 minutes; set aside. Mix coating ingredients. Dip cutlets in beaten egg, then in coating. Place in 12×8-in. baking dish. Cover with wax paper. Microwave 8 to 10 minutes, or until surface is no longer pink and cutlets are tender, rearranging after half the cooking time. (Do not turn over.) Drain.

Top each cutlet with ¼ of mozarella cheese. Pour sauce over and sprinkle with Parmesan. Cover with wax paper. Microwave 4 to 6 minutes or until mozarella melts and sauce is hot.

How to Microwave Veal & Dumplings

Measure flour and seasonings into paper or plastic bag. One at a time, shake cutlets in bag to coat.

Place butter in 12×8-in. dish. Microwave at High 2 minutes, or until very hot. Add cutlets and onion quarters. Cover with plastic wrap. Microwave at High 2 minutes.

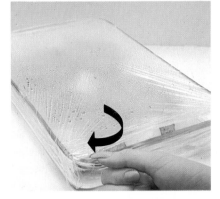

Reduce power to 50% (Medium). Microwave 10 to 12 minutes, or until veal is tender, rotating dish ½ turn after half the time. Let stand while preparing dumplings.

Combine flour, baking powder and seasonings in a small bowl. In 1-cup measure, mix together milk, egg and butter. Blend into flour mixture. (If batter is too stiff, add another teaspoon of milk.)

Drop batter by rounded tablespoonfuls into bread crumbs. Roll to coat; set aside.

Combine soup and mushrooms in small bowl. Pour over veal. Cover. Microwave at High 4 minutes, or until hot. Top with dumplings. Microwave 5 to 6 minutes, or until dumplings are firm to the touch.

Pork

Pork ranks second only to beef in popularity with American cooks. It's a versatile meat; fresh or smoked, it can be cooked, seasoned and served in a variety of dishes.

Fresh pork roasts, chops, ribs and cubes all have their own distinctive appearance and can be prepared in different ways. Curing and smoking change the character of pork completely. In addition to popular ham and bacon, try smoked, butt, chops or Canadian-style bacon.

Fresh pork should be thoroughly cooked, but not over-cooked. Pork releases moisture quickly, so the dividing line between cooked and

over-cooked is critical. Studies show that pork is safe to eat and more juicy and tender when it is served at a finished temperature of 170°. Smaller cuts should be fork-tender with slightly pink juices. Standing time is important because it allows pork to cook completely without drying out.

In this book, recipes for smoked meats have been developed with national brands. Local or home cures may be even more flavorful, but differ in the amount of salt and sugar used for curing. Sugar attracts microwave energy and salt promotes drying, so watch these cures carefully. Shield, turn over, rotate or stir meat frequently to avoid over-cooking or drying.

Know Your Pork

Pork varies across the country, depending on the breed of hog raised and the methods used. Hogs which are penned and corn-fed will be the most tender. Names for pork chops are confusing. Depending on where you live, a "Center Cut Chop" may be any one of three different chops. Since all chops are microwaved the same way, the chart on the right lists only the standard names.

In the South, most of the pork is cured or smoked. Every area has a local specialty, generally ham or bacon. These home cures are often more flavorful than national brands, but they vary in the amount of salt and sugar used for curing. Be guided by conventional cooking methods; lower the power level or watch carefully, since both salt and sugar influence microwaving.

Chart at right shows popular retail cuts of pork and the wholesale cuts from which they are taken. It was adapted for microwaving from information supplied by the National Livestock and Meat Board. Ground pork and sausages are made from several cuts and have been omitted because they are easy to identify.

How to Select Fresh Pork

Fat makes pork tender, juicy and flavorful. If you don't care to eat it, trim it after cooking.

Marbling is as important for pork tenderness as it is for beef. Good pork is pink or rosy in color and has a fine grain. The exterior fat should be firm and white. Avoid pork with crumbly, milky colored fat and excessive surface moisture. Paper liner under pre-packaged meat makes it hard to judge, but check for oozing juices.

How to Select Cured or Smoked Pork

Select cured pork which is marbled, fine grained and has a good layer of exterior fat. Color should be pink, but will turn grey when exposed to light. Quality is not affected.

Avoid extremes. Hams shoud not appear either watery or dried out with visible fibers. "Water added" hams microwave well.

How Much Pork to Buy

Cut	Amount per Serving
Boneless	¼-⅓ pound
Bone-in, chops, roasts, hams	½-¾ pound
Bony ribs, hocks	1 pound

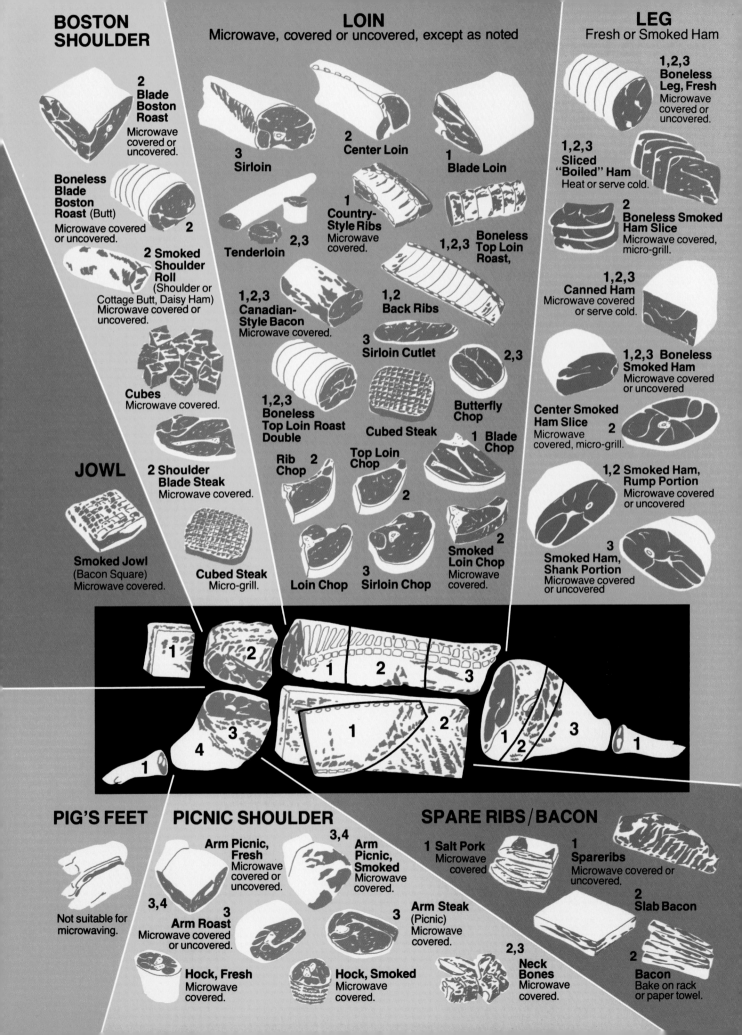

BOSTON SHOULDER

2 Blade Boston Roast
Microwave covered or uncovered.

Boneless Blade Boston Roast (Butt)
Microwave covered or uncovered.

2 Smoked Shoulder Roll
(Shoulder or Cottage Butt, Daisy Ham)
Microwave covered or uncovered.

Cubes
Microwave covered.

2 Shoulder Blade Steak
Microwave covered.

JOWL

Smoked Jowl
(Bacon Square)
Microwave covered.

Cubed Steak
Micro-grill.

LOIN
Microwave, covered or uncovered, except as noted

3 Sirloin

2 Center Loin

1 Blade Loin

Tenderloin 2,3

1 Country-Style Ribs
Microwave covered.

1,2,3 Canadian-Style Bacon
Microwave covered.

1,2 Back Ribs

1,2,3 Boneless Top Loin Roast,

3 Sirloin Cutlet

2,3 Butterfly Chop

1,2,3 Boneless Top Loin Roast Double

Cubed Steak

1 Blade Chop

Rib Chop 2

Top Loin Chop

2 Smoked Loin Chop
Microwave covered.

Loin Chop 3

3 Sirloin Chop

LEG
Fresh or Smoked Ham

1,2,3 Boneless Leg, Fresh
Microwave covered or uncovered.

1,2,3 Sliced "Boiled" Ham
Heat or serve cold.

2 Boneless Smoked Ham Slice
Microwave covered, micro-grill.

1,2,3 Canned Ham
Microwave covered or serve cold.

1,2,3 Boneless Smoked Ham
Microwave covered or uncovered

Center Smoked Ham Slice
Microwave covered, micro-grill. 2

1,2 Smoked Ham, Rump Portion
Microwave covered or uncovered

3 Smoked Ham, Shank Portion
Microwave covered or uncovered

PIG'S FEET

Not suitable for microwaving.

PICNIC SHOULDER

Arm Picnic, Fresh
Microwave covered or uncovered. 3,4

3,4 Arm Picnic, Smoked
Microwave covered.

3,4 Arm Roast
Microwave covered or uncovered. 3

Hock, Fresh
Microwave covered.

3 Arm Steak
(Picnic)
Microwave covered.

Hock, Smoked
Microwave covered.

SPARE RIBS/BACON

1 Salt Pork
Microwave covered

1 Spareribs
Microwave covered or uncovered.

2 Slab Bacon

2,3 Neck Bones
Microwave covered.

2 Bacon
Bake on rack or paper towel.

How to Store Pork

Fresh and cured pork should be stored in the meat keeper or the coldest part of the refrigerator. Pre-packaged pork may be frozen in the original wrappings for 1 to 2 weeks. For longer storage, wrap in freezer paper as shown on page 17.

How to Store Fresh Pork

Pre-packaged pork may be stored in the original wrapping, but will keep best if you rewrap as described at right.

Unwrap pork packaged in butcher's paper. Remove tray and liner from pre-packaged pork. Place meat in a covered dish, heavy-duty plastic bag, or wrap loosely in freezer paper or plastic wrap.

How to Store Cured Pork

Refrigerate film-wrapped ham and bacon in the original package for 1 to 2 weeks.

Check label on canned ham carefully. Unless it states specifically that the ham may be kept at room temperature, store in refrigerator.

Pork Storage Chart

Cut	Refrigerator (40°F.)	Freezer Compartment	Freezer (under −0°)
Fresh Pork	2 days	No more than 1 week, unless you are sure temperature is below 0°. Defrosting times in this book are based on 0° freezer temperature.	3-6 months
Ground Pork	1 day		1-3 months
Smoked Ham, whole	1 week		2 months
Canned Ham	3 months		Not recommended
Ham Slice, Smoked Pork Chops	3-4 days		2 months
Bacon	1 week		Not recommended

How to Take Advantage of Good Pork Buys

Supermarkets feature pork frequently. If a roast is too large for your family, you needn't eat leftovers all week. Cut up the meat for several different meals or freeze some of it in single serving or family-size packages.

How to Divide Fresh Pork Roasts

Boston shoulder roast makes three different meals. Cut off the end containing the blade bone for use as a pork roast. Slice the remaining section into boneless pork steaks and cube the small end for use in casseroles.

Pork loin is often sold already cut into a roast and chops. Use some now and freeze the rest for future use.

How to Divide Hams

Shank half of a ham can be cut up for three meals. Ask the butcher to saw off the shank end for soup. Divide the rest yourself into a bone-in ham for baking and boneless slices or cubes.

Small canned ham is a good buy for a small household. A 1½-lb. ham yields 5 to 6 servings as baked slices and cubes.

Pork Defrosting Chart

Cut	Comments	50% (Medium) Min./Lb.	30% (Low) Min./Lb.
Loin Roasts	Follow directions for large roasts, page 20.	6¼-8¼	10½-13¾
Tenderloin	Follow directions for beef tenderloin, page 20.	5-7	8½-11¾
Chops	Follow directions for small steaks, page 21.	3½-6	6-10
Cubes and Strips	Follow directions, page 23.	4-6	6¾-10
Ground Pork	Follow directions for ground beef, page 22.	2¾-5	5-8½

Pork Roasts

Pork dries out quickly once it passes the "just done" stage. To assure a succulent roast, use a sensor. Before inserting a sensor into a bone-in roast, examine the meat to determine the position of the bones. Knowing where the bones are will also help when you carve the roast.

Fresh ham and tenderloin are neither smoked nor cured. They are available in some Northern states.

	Approx. Total Time: Min./Lb.	Start at High Power	Finish at 50% (Med.)	Remove at Internal Temp.
Pork Loin, Bone-in, or Boneless	12-16	first 5 min.	7-11	165°
Fresh Ham	13½-16½	first 5 min.	8½-11½	165°
Tenderloin	12½-16½	first 3 min.	9½-13½	165°

How to Microwave Fresh Pork Loin & Ham

Rub roast with cut clove of garlic or crumbled herbs, if desired. Insert microwave thermometer, if used.

Place roast, fattiest side down, on roasting rack. Estimate the total roasting time and divide in half.

Microwave at High 5 minutes. Reduce power to 50% (Medium). Microwave remaining part of first half of time.

How to Microwave Pork Tenderloin

Shield meat over ends and 1-in. down sides. Insert thermometer, if used, as directed for beef tenderloin, page 28.

Place meat on rack in 12×8-in. dish. Estimate the total cooking time; divide in half.

Microwave 3 minutes at High. Reduce power to 50% (Medium). Microwave remaining part of first half of time.

How to Insert Microwave Thermometer or Probe

Boneless Loin, Rib End and Center Cut Roasts. Insert sensor so tip is in the center of the meatiest area. (but not touching fat.)

Loin End Roast and Ham. From round-bone end of loin roast or side of ham, insert sensor into the meatiest area until it touches the bone. Withdraw sensor until the tip is in center of meaty area.

Turn roast over, fat side up. (If using probe, insert at this time.)

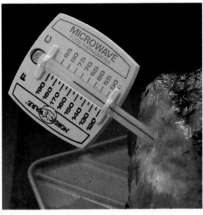

Microwave for second half of time, or until roast reaches 165°.

Tent loosely with foil. Let stand 5 to 10 minutes, until internal temperature registers 170°.

Remove shielding. Turn roast over. Insert probe, if used.

Spread ½ cup chunky applesauce over roast if desired. Microwave until the internal temperature reaches 165°.

Tent loosely with foil. Let stand until temperature reaches 170°, about 5 to 10 minutes.

Crown Roast of Pork

A crown roast makes a dramatic party presentation, and is easy to microwave. Order it from your butcher several days in advance. He will form a pork loin roast into a circle and remove the back-bone for easy carving.

If serving Bread or Rice Stuffing, prepare it before you start to microwave the roast. If you pre-fer a vegetable garnish, micro-wave it while roast is standing.

Suggested fillings are: Sliced mushrooms or apples micro-waved in butter, mixed peas, onions and mushrooms, mixed corn, onion and green pepper, instant mashed potatoes with butter and chopped parsley.

Start at High
First 5 min.

Finish at 50% (Medium)
15-17 min. per lb.

Rice Stuffing

½ pound fresh sausage meat
2 stalks celery, thinly sliced
1 large onion, chopped
8 oz. fresh mushrooms, sliced
2 cups cooked rice
1 tablespoon parsley flakes
1 teaspoon salt
½ teaspoon rosemary leaves, crushed
⅛ teaspoon pepper

Crumble sausage into a 2-qt. casserole. Microwave at High 2 to 3 minutes, or until meat is set. Break up with fork and set aside on paper towel.

Drain fat from casserole. Add celery, onion and mushrooms; cover. Microwave 5 to 6 min-utes, or until onion is translu-cent. Stir in reserved sausage and remaining ingredients.

Bread Stuffing

½ cup chopped dried apricots
¼ cup water
1 lb. fresh pork sausage meat
2 stalks celery, thinly sliced
1 large onion, chopped
2 tablespoons butter or margarine
2 cups herb seasoned stuffing mix
1 cup hot water
1 tablespoon parsley flakes
1½ teaspoons seasoned salt
1 teaspoon instant chicken bouillon granules

Combine apricots and water in small bowl. Microwave at High 3 minutes. Stir and set aside.

Crumble sausage into 2-qt. casserole. Microwave 4 to 5 minutes, or until meat is set. Break up with fork; set aside on paper towel.

Drain fat from casserole. Add celery, onion and butter. Micro-wave 4 to 5 minutes, or until onion is translucent. Stir in apricot mixture, sausage and remaining ingredients.

Variation:
Substitute 1 cup chopped, dried apples for apricots and increase water to ⅓ cup.

How to Microwave a Crown Roast of Pork

Prepare Bread or Rice Stuffing, if desired. Set aside.

Insert thermometer, if used, between 2 ribs, so tip is in meaty area on inside of crown and does not touch fat or bone. Place roast on rack with bony ends down.

Estimate total cooking time; divide in half. Microwave at High first 5 minutes. Reduce power to 50% (Medium). Microwave remainder of first half of time.

Turn roast over, rib ends up. Insert temperature probe, if used. Microwave until approximately ½ hour of cooking time remains.

Fill cavity lightly with stuffing. Place remaining stuffing around roast. When Rice Stuffing is used, fit wax paper over stuffing to prevent excess browning.

Microwave remaining time, or until internal temperature reaches 165°.

Tent roast loosely with foil. Let stand 10 minutes, or until temperature reaches 170°.

Remove roast to serving plate, using spatula to support stuffing.

Decorate rib ends with paper frills or spiced crab apples. To serve, carve down between chops.

Ribs

Spare ribs can be microwaved in 2 ways, depending on your tastes. Dry-roasted ribs are covered with wax paper to prevent spatters, and are chewy, finger food. Braised ribs are tightly covered and steamed in liquid so they almost slip off the bones.

Since ribs are bony, you will need ¾ to 1-lb. per person. The most important step in microwaving them is arranging, and rearranging them in the dish. Enough rib pieces to feed 3 to 4 people should be laid against the sides of the dish and overlapped slightly on the bottom. When rearranging, expose the least cooked portions and overlap the most cooked pieces.

Roasted Ribs

2½ to 3-lb. spare ribs, cut in 2 to
    3-rib pieces
1 onion, thinly sliced
½ teaspoon basil
1 cup bottled barbecue sauce
2 teaspoons lemon juice

                Serves 3 to 4

Braised Ribs

2½ to 3-lbs. spare ribs, cut in
    2 to 3-rib pieces
1 onion, thinly sliced
½ teaspoon basil
1 lemon, thinly sliced
1 cup water
1 cup bottled barbecue sauce

              Serves 3 to 4

Sweet-and-Sour Sauce

Prepare sauce before microwaving ribs by either the roasted or braised method. After draining liquid, substitute this for barbecue sauce.

¼ cup brown sugar
1 tablespoon cornstarch
½ cup pineapple juice
¼ cup vinegar
2 tablespoons soy sauce

In a 2-cup measure, combine brown sugar and cornstarch. Measure in remaining ingredients; stir well. Microwave at High 3 to 4 minutes, or until thick and translucent, stirring every minute.

Start at High	Roasted Finish at 50% (Medium)	Braised Finish at 50% (Medium)
first 5 min.	25-35 min.	30-40 min.

How To Microwave Barbecued Ribs

Arrange ribs around sides and over bottom of 12×8-in. dish or 3-qt. casserole, overlapping slightly as needed. Spread with onion rings. Sprinkle with basil.

Roasted Ribs. Cover with wax paper, which prevents spatters without steaming ribs.

Braised Ribs. Add lemon slices and water. Cover tightly with lid or plastic wrap.

84

Pennsylvania Ribs and Kraut

2½ to 3-lbs. ribs, cut in
    2 to 3 rib pieces
  2 tablespoons each bouquet
    sauce and water, combined
  1 can (27-oz.) sauerkraut,
    drained
  1 medium onion, chopped
  1 medium apple, peeled and
    finely chopped
  2 tablespoons brown sugar
  1 teaspoon caraway seeds
    (optional)

Serves 3 to 4

Arrange ribs around sides and over bottom of a 3-qt. casserole, overlapping slightly as needed. Cover tightly. Microwave at High 5 minutes. Reduce power to 50% (Medium). Microwave 15 minutes.

Remove ribs. Brush with bouquet sauce mixture; set aside. Drain liquid from casserole.

Combine sauerkraut, onion, apple, brown sugar and caraway seed in casserole. Arrange ribs on top. Cover. Microwave 15 to 25 minutes, until ribs are fork tender and sauerkraut is heated through.

Microwave at High 5 minutes. Reduce power to 50% (Medium). Microwave for half the cooking time. Rearrange and turn ribs over, so least cooked pieces are exposed, and more cooked parts are overlapped. Re-cover.

Microwave remaining time or until fork tender. Drain liquid. Add sauce (and lemon juice for roasted ribs). Microwave uncovered 4 to 6 minutes.

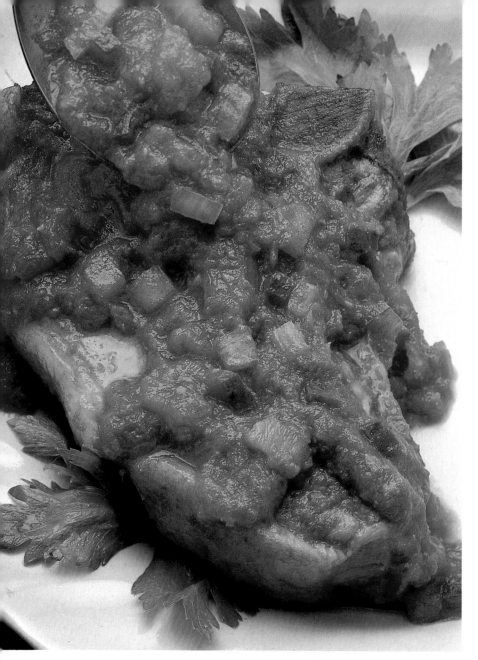

Pork Chops

Pork chops dry out rapidly unless care is taken to keep them moist. Seal the surface with crumbs, mask the chops with sauce or microwave them tightly covered. Thick pork chops are more juicy and tender than thin ones because they have less opportunity to lose moisture.

French Deli Style Pork Chops

This is a microwave version of the ready-cooked chops which are a specialty of French butcher shops. The sauce provides moisture, while pickle and vinegar give a piquant flavor.

4 pork chops, 1-in. thick
½ cup water
1 tablespoon flour
1 teaspoon instant beef bouillon
2 fresh tomatoes, peeled, seeded and chopped
1 medium onion, chopped
1 can (6-oz.) tomato paste
1 tablespoon chopped dill pickle
1 tablespoon vinegar
½ teaspoon salt
¼ teaspoon pepper

Serves 4

How To Microwave French Deli Style Pork Chops

Arrange chops in a 12×8-in. dish with meatiest portions to outside. Set aside.

Measure water into a 1-qt. measure. Stir in flour and bouillon, then remaining ingredients. Pour sauce over chops. Cover with wax paper.

Microwave at 50% (Medium) 25 to 35 minutes, or until meat next to bone has lost its pink color, turning chops over after half the cooking time.

Onion Pork Chops

We do not recommend frying chops either conventionally or on a microwave browning grill because they dry out and toughen in the time needed to cook them through.

The onions in this recipe flavor the pork chops and provide moisture to make them tender.

4 pork chops, 1-in. thick
¼ cup seasoned bread crumbs, spread on wax paper
1 tablespoon salad oil
1 teaspoon salt
¼ teaspoon pepper
2 medium onions, thinly sliced

Serves 4

How To Microwave Onion Pork Chops

Dredge chops in crumbs, pressing meat down to make crumbs adhere. Set aside.

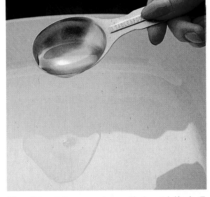

Preheat browning dish at High 5 minutes, then add oil and tilt dish so bottom is coated.

Place chops in dish; microwave at High 1 minute. Turn chops over; microwave 1 minute.

Arrange chops with meatiest portions to outside of dish. Season with salt and pepper. Spread onion slices over chops.

Cover. Reduce power to 50% (Medium) and microwave 20 to 30 minutes, or until meat next to bone has lost its pink color.

Turn chops over after half the cooking time and replace onions on top.

Stuffed Pork Chops

4 pork chops, 1-in. thick
Stuffing (below)
½ cup fine, dry bread crumbs
    spread on wax paper

Make pockets in chops follow-ing directions below. Prepare stuffing. Fill each chop with ¼ of stuffing and secure open edges with wooden picks.

Dredge chops in bread crumbs, pressing meat lightly so crumbs adhere.

Arrange chops in 8×8-in. or 12×8-in. dish, with meatiest portions to outside. Cover with wax paper. Microwave at 50% (Medium) 15 minutes.

Turn chops over; re-cover. Microwave 10 to 20 minutes, or until meat next to bone has lost its pink color.

How To Stuff Pork Chops

Make a pocket by slicing chop horizontally with a sharp knife. Cut deeply enough to touch the bone, leaving a 1-in. border at sides of chop.

Fill pocket with ¼ of stuffing. Secure open edges with wooden picks, placed diagonally, so ends do not extend beyond surface of chop. Dredge chop in bread crumbs.

Mushroom Stuffing

1 cup sliced mushrooms
½ cup chopped onion
2 tablespoons butter or
    margarine
⅛ to ¼ teaspoon crumbled
    thyme
1½ cups herb-seasoned
    stuffing mix
½ cup hot tap water

Stuffs 4 Pork Chops

In a 1-qt. measure, combine mushrooms, onion and butter. Microwave at High 2 to 4 minutes, or until onions are tender-crisp. Add thyme and stuffing mix; toss to combine.

Measure water into a 1-cup measure. Microwave at High 45 to 60 seconds, or until water boils. Stir into stuffing.

Pork Strips & Chunks

Cut your own pork strips and cubes from a butt roast (page 79), or a few chops. If you buy blade steak, be sure to allow for bone and fat so you will have enough lean meat for the recipe.

Creamy Pork & Peas

1 tablespoon cooking oil
1 lb. boneless pork, cut in ¼ × 1-in. strips
1 pkg. (10-oz.) frozen peas, defrosted in pkg. at High 3 to 4 min.
1 can (10¾-oz.) cream of celery soup
⅛ teaspoon pepper

Serves 3 to 4

Preheat browning dish as manufacturer directs. Add oil; tilt dish to coat bottom. Stir in pork. Microwave at High 1 minute . Stir; microwave 2 minutes.

Mix in peas, soup and pepper. Reduce power to 50% (Medium). Microwave 15 to 20 minutes, until pork is no longer pink in center, stirring after half the time.

Sweet & Sour Pork ▼

¼ cup brown sugar
2 tablespoons cornstarch
¼ cup cider vinegar
2 tablespoons soy sauce
1 can (8¼-oz.) pineapple chunks, drained and juice reserved
1 lb. boneless pork, cut in ½ to ¾-in. cubes
1 can (5-oz.) water chestnuts, drained and sliced
1 medium green pepper, cut in ¼-in. strips
½ chopped onion

Serves 4

Combine sugar and cornstarch in 1½ to 2-qt. casserole. Stir in vinegar, soy sauce and pineapple juice. Add pork. Cover.

Microwave at High 2 minutes. Reduce power to 50% (Medium). Microwave 10 to 15 minutes, or until pork is no longer pink in center, stirring once or twice.

Add water chestnuts, green pepper and onion. Cover. Microwave 4 to 6 minutes until pepper is tender-crisp, stirring once during cooking. Mix in pineapple chunks. Serve over rice or fried noodles.

Savory Pork Stew

4 slices bacon, each cut in 6 pieces
1 lb. boneless pork, cut in ½ to ¾-in. cubes
¼ cup flour
1 large onion, thinly sliced
1½ cups thinly sliced carrots
1 cup thinly sliced celery
1 can (16-oz.) cream style corn
½ cup water
1 tablespoon chicken bouillon granules
1 bay leaf
1 teaspoon parsley flakes
½ teaspoon salt
½ teaspoon bouquet sauce
¼ teaspoon marjoram
⅛ teaspoon pepper

Serves 4

Place bacon in 3-qt. casserole; cover. Microwave at High 3 minutes. Drain fat. Add pork. Sprinkle with flour and toss to coat. Add remaining ingredients. Cover tightly.

Microwave at High 5 minutes. Reduce power to 50% (Medium). Microwave 30 to 40 minutes, or until pork is no longer pink in center, stirring after half the cooking time. Let stand 5 minutes.

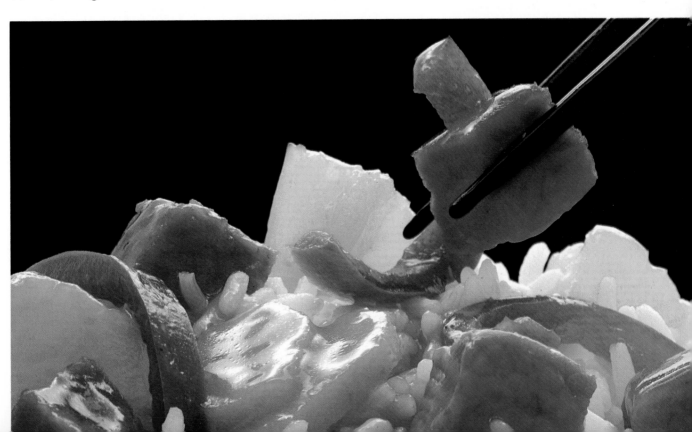

Ham

Ham is available in many forms. Canned hams and boneless, rolled hams are fully cooked and ready to eat, although their flavor improves with heating. Bone-in hams may be labeled either "fully cooked" or "cook before eating". If the ham is not labeled, it is probably a "cook before eating" ham.

"Picnic hams" are cut from the shoulder, rather than the hind leg of pork, and contain more fat and tissue. They are available bone-in and boneless, fully cooked and "cook before eating". Many fully cooked picnic hams are not labeled, so it is best to check with the butcher. Either type of picnic shoulder should be microwaved tightly covered to tenderize it.

Canned & Boneless Rolled Ham 50% (Medium)	Approx. Min./Lb.	Removal Temp.
Canned Ham	6-8	130°
Boneless, rolled ham	10-15	130°

How to Prepare Ham for Microwaving

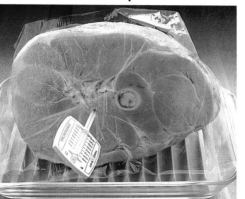

Bone-in Ham, fully cooked. Place on rack. Cover cut surface with plastic wrap. Shield, if used, must be at least 3-in. from top of oven. Insert thermometer into center of meatiest area, not touching fat or bone.

Bone-in Ham, "cook before eating". Place ham in cooking bag or tightly covered dish. Insert microwave thermometer, if used, into meatiest area, not touching fat or bone.

Picnic Ham. Place ham in cooking bag. If ham contains bones, check their position with a skewer before inserting microwave thermometer in meatiest area.

How to Microwave Bone-in Hams and Picnic Hams

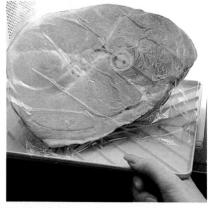

Estimate the total cooking time and divide in half. Microwave at High 5 minutes. Reduce power to 50% (Medium). Microwave remaining part of first half of time.

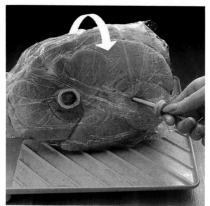

Turn ham over. Insert probe, if used. Microwave second half of cooking time, or until internal temperature reaches removal time indicated on chart.

Let stand, loosely tented with foil, 10 minutes. Temperature will rise 5° to 10°.

Bone-in & Picnic Hams

	Approx. Min./Lb.	Start at High Power	Finish at 50% (Medium)
Bone-in, fully cooked	11½-14½	first 5 min.	130°
Bone-in, cook before eating	15-18	first 5 min.	160°
Picnic Shoulder fully cooked	15-18	first 5 min.	130°
Picnic Shoulder cook before eating	15½-18½	first 5 min.	160°

Ham Glazes

For a colorful sheen and added flavor, spread one of these glazes on ham during the last 10 to 15 minutes of cooking time.

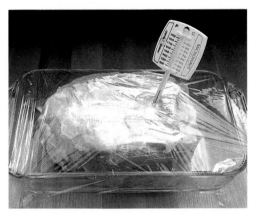

Canned Ham. Place in baking dish; cover with vented plastic wrap. Insert microwave thermometer, if used, through plastic so tip is in center of meat.

Boneless Ham, fully cooked. Place ham in baking dish. Cover cut surface with plastic wrap, or cover dish. Insert microwave thermometer, if used, so tip is in center of meat. Shield upper cut edge with foil, if desired.

Cranberry Glaze

¾ cup apple juice
1 tablespoon cornstarch
1 can (8-oz.) whole cranberry sauce
¼ cup barbecue sauce

In a 2-cup measure, blend cornstarch into apple juice. Stir in remaining ingredients. Microwave at High 4 to 6 minutes, until cranberry sauce dissolves and glaze is slightly thickened, stirring once during cooking.

How to Microwave Canned or Boneless Rolled Ham

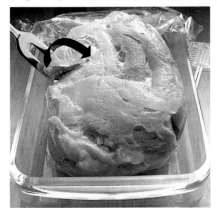

Microwave at 50% (Medium) for half the estimated cooking time. Turn ham over. Insert probe, if used. Replace shielding, if used, on top edge of ham.

Microwave remaining time, or until internal temperature reaches 130°. Let stand, tented with foil, 5 to 10 minutes.

Savory Apricot Glaze

1 cup apricot preserves
1 bottle (8-oz.) Russian Dressing
1 envelope onion gravy mix

Combine all ingredients in a 1-qt. measure. Microwave at High 3 to 5 minutes, or until jelly dissolves.

Mustard Glaze

¾ cup packed brown sugar
3 tablespoons prepared mustard

Combine sugar and mustard in small bowl.

Ham Slices

Ham slices may be fully cooked or "cook before eating", but often are not labeled.

Ham Slice & Scalloped Potatoes

1 box (5½-oz.) scalloped
   potato mix
2 lb. fully cooked ham slice,
   cut 1½-in. thick

Serves 4 to 6

In 12×8-in. dish, mix scalloped potatoes as directed on package, reducing water by ¾ cup. Cover with wax paper. Microwave at High 10 minutes. Stir. Slash fat on ham slice. Arrange ham on top of potatoes. Cover with wax paper. Microwave at 50% (Medium) 15 to 20 minutes, or until ham is hot and potatoes tender, rotating dish ½ turn after half the time.

Honey Glazed Ham Slice

2 lb. fully cooked ham slice,
   cut 1½-in. thick

Glaze:
¼ cup honey
 2 tablespoons orange juice
 1 tablespoon vinegar
 1 teaspoon cornstarch

Serves 6

How to Microwave Honey Glazed Ham Slice

Combine glaze ingredients in a 2-cup measure. Microwave at High 1½ to 2 minutes, or until slightly thickened, stirring after first minute. Set aside.

Slash fat on ham slice. Place ham in 12×8-in. dish; cover with wax paper. Reduce power to 50% (Medium). Microwave 10 minutes. Drain.

Pour glaze over ham. Do not cover. Microwave at 50% (Medium) 7 to 10 minutes, or until ham is hot.

Smoked Pork Chops

These recipes are for fully cooked chops. If your chops are "cook before eating", add 2 to 4 more minutes microwaving time.

Barbecued Smoked Chops

4 fully cooked, smoked pork chops
½ cup barbecue sauce, divided

Serves 4

Arrange chops on roasting rack in 12×8-in. dish, with meatiest portions to outside. Top with half of sauce. Microwave at High 5 minutes. Turn chops over. Spread with remaining sauce. Microwave 3 to 5 minutes, or until chops are heated through.

Cheddar Chops

1 can (16-oz.) lima beans, drained
2 tablespoons instant minced onion
4 fully cooked, smoked pork chops
4 slices pineapple (optional)
1 cup shredded cheddar or American cheese

Serves 4

How to Microwave Cheddar Chops

Combine beans and onion in 12×8-in. dish. Arrange chops over beans with meatiest portions to outside of dish. Cover with wax paper. Microwave at High 5 minutes.

Turn chops over; re-cover. Microwave 3 to 5 minutes, or until chops are heated through. Top each chop with pineapple slice, if desired.

Sprinkle shredded cheese over casserole. Re-cover. Reduce power to 50% (Medium). Microwave 3 to 5 minutes, or until cheese melts.

Canadian-Style Bacon

Canadian-style bacon is the boneless eye of loin which is shaped into a compact roll and cured and smoked like ham. Thin slices of fully cooked Canadian bacon can be heated rapidly with a covering of wax paper. Larger pieces need water and a tight cover because the meat is defatted and tends to dry out.

Canadian Bacon Chunks

	Approx. Min./Lb.	Start at High	Finish at 50% (Medium)
1-2 lbs.	11-15	3	130°
Over 2 lbs.	11-15	5	130°

Canadian Bacon Slices

¼-in. thick slices	High Power	Rotate ¼ turn
2	¾-1¼ min.	Not needed
4	1½-2½ min.	After 1 min.
6	2½-3½ min.	After 1½ min.
8	3-3½ min.	After 1½ min.

How to Microwave Canadian Bacon Chunks

Remove casing. Place bacon in baking dish; add ¼ cup water. Insert microwave thermometer, if desired, so tip is in center of meat. Cover with vented plastic wrap.

Estimate the total cooking time and divide in half. Microwave at High according to chart above. Reduce power to 50% (Medium). Microwave remaining part of first half of time.

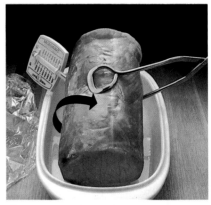

Turn bacon over. Microwave remaining time or until internal temperature reaches 130°. Let stand, covered, 10 minutes.

How to Microwave Canadian Bacon Slices

Slice bacon ¼-in. thick. Arrange on plate in single layer. Cover with wax paper.

Microwave according to chart, rotating dish ¼ turn when heating more than 2 slices. Popping noise during heating is normal.

Regular Bacon

Arrange bacon on 3 layers of paper towel or on a rack in baking dish; cover with paper towel. Microwave at High ¾ to 1 minute per slice, until bacon looks slightly underdone. Let stand 3 to 5 minutes to brown and crisp.

Ham Loaf

The mixture used for ham loaf is more moist than a basic ground beef meatloaf. Microwave ham loaf at High to get it started, then reduce power to 50% (Medium) to prevent drying and over-cooking on edges.

Pineapple Upside-down Loaf ▶

Loaf:
¾ lb. ground ham
¾ lb. ground pork
½ cup dry bread crumbs
½ cup milk
¼ cup chopped onion
¼ cup chopped celery
2 eggs
¾ teaspoon dry mustard
¼ teaspoon pepper

Topping:
4 teaspoons brown sugar
1 can (8¼-oz.) pineapple slices

Glaze:
Reserved pineapple juice
2 teaspoons cornstarch

Serves 4 to 6

Combine loaf ingredients well. Set aside.

Sprinkle brown sugar evenly over bottom of 9×5-in. loaf dish. Drain pineapple juice into 1 cup measure. Set aside. Arrange pineapple slices over brown sugar in bottom of dish.

Press loaf mixture into dish evenly. Microwave at High 5 minutes. Reduce power to 50% (Medium). Microwave 23 to 28 minutes, or until loaf is firm and center is set (internal temperature 160°), rotating dish ½ turn after half the time. Drain loaf, turn out on serving dish. Let stand tented loosely with foil while making glaze.

Add water to reserved pineapple juice to make ½ cup. Stir in cornstarch until dissolved. Microwave at High 1 to 2½ minutes, or until thickened. Pour glaze over loaf.

Traditional Ham Loaf

Loaf:
¾ lb. ground ham
¾ lb. ground pork
⅓ cup chopped onion
⅓ cup dry bread crumbs
¼ cup milk
2 eggs
1 tablespoon prepared mustard
1½ teaspoons parsley flakes
½ teaspoon pepper

Topping:
¼ cup packed brown sugar
4 tablespoons pineapple juice, divided
1 teaspoon prepared mustard

Serves 4 to 6

Mix loaf ingredients together thoroughly. Press evenly into a 9×5-in. loaf dish. In a 1-cup measure, combine sugar, 1 tablespoon pineapple juice and mustard. Spread over loaf and sprinkle with remaining pineapple juice.

Microwave at High 5 minutes. Reduce power to 50% (Medium). Microwave 23 to 28 minutes, or until loaf is firm and center is set (internal temperature 160°), rotating dish ½ turn after half the cooking time.

Using spatulas, lift loaf from dish to serving plate. Let stand, tented loosely with foil, 5 minutes.

Pork & Ham Leftovers

Golden Pork Casserole

½ cup chopped onion
½ medium green pepper,
   chopped
¼ cup chopped celery
2 cups cooked pork, ½-in. cubes
1 can (10¾-oz.) cream of
   mushroom soup
1 envelope chicken with rice
   soup mix
1 cup quick-cooking rice

Serves 4

Combine vegetables in 2-qt. casserole. Cover. Microwave at High 3 to 4 minutes, or until tender. Stir in remaining ingredients. Cover. Microwave 9 to 12 minutes, or until rice is cooked, stirring after half the cooking time.

◄ Ham & Broccoli Casserole

2 pkgs. (8-oz.) frozen broccoli
   spears
2 cups cooked ham, ½-in. cubes
1 can (3-oz.) French fried
   onion rings, divided
1 cup shredded cheddar cheese
1 can (10¾-oz.) cream of
   mushroom soup
¼ cup milk

Serves 4 to 6

How to Microwave Ham & Broccoli Casserole

Place both broccoli packages in oven. Microwave at High 5 minutes. Drain broccoli well, and arrange in 12×8-in. dish, alternating heads and stems.

Top with ham, half the onion rings and cheese. Blend soup and milk. Pour over casserole. Cover with wax paper. Microwave at High 8 to 10 minutes, or until broccoli is tender-crisp.

Sprinkle with remaining onion rings. Microwave, uncovered, 5 to 6 minutes, or until casserole is heated through.

Ham & Cheese Ring

Assemble this dish the night before and microwave the following day.

    6 slices white bread
    ¼ cup chopped onion
    2 cups cooked ham, ½-in.
        cubes
    1 cup shredded cheddar
        cheese
    4 eggs
    1 cup milk
    ½ teaspoon salt
    ⅛ teaspoon pepper
    ⅛ teaspoon dry mustard
    2 teaspoons parsley flakes
                    Serves 4 to 6

Cut bread into ½-in. cubes. Place ¾ of cubes in bottom of ring mold. Top with onion, ham, cheese and remaining bread.

In small bowl, blend together eggs, milk, salt, pepper and mustard. Pour over layers; sprinkle with parsley. Cover. Let stand, refrigerated, overnight.

Microwave, uncovered, at 50% (Medium) 23 to 28 minutes, or until set, rotating ½ turn after half the time. Let stand 5 minutes.

Pork & Candied Yams

    2 cups thin strips of cooked
        pork
    1 tablespoon flour
    1 cup finely chopped apple
    1 can (23-oz.) yams in syrup,
        drained and cut in 1-in.
        cubes
    1 tablespoon butter or margarine
    ¼ cup brown sugar
    ⅓ cup coarsely chopped pecans
                        Serves 4

Toss pork with flour in a 1-qt. casserole. Top with apple, then yams. Dot with butter. Sprinkle with sugar and pecans, cover.

Microwave at High 8 to 11 minutes, or until apples are tender and casserole is heated through, rotating dish ½ turn after half the cooking time.

97

Lamb

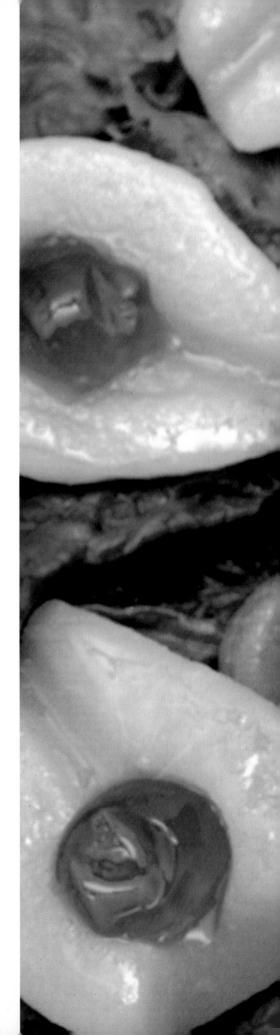

Lamb is a seasonal meat. Some form of lamb is available all year, but the choicest young lamb is most plentiful and reasonably priced during spring and early summer. The best ways to determine the age of lamb are the color of the meat, condition of the bone and size or weight of the leg.

Milk-fed baby or "hot house" lamb is difficult to obtain except in large cities with ethnic markets. The lean meat is pink; the bones are porous and red; an average leg weighs 3 to 4 pounds.

"Spring" lamb is a confusing term. Some butchers use it to designate any lamb which is under a year old. Others reserve the name, spring, for young lamb and market heavier, older animals simply as "lamb". To add to the confusion, a few lambs are born throughout the year, so some genuine spring lamb is available in the fall and winter.

Young spring lamb has dark pink flesh and porous red bones; the leg weighs 4½ to 5½ pounds. Average or fall lamb has light red flesh, porous red bones and a leg weighs 6 to 7 pounds.

Yearling lamb or young mutton is marketed in winter and early spring. The lean is medium-red and the bones are white. A full leg weighs 7 to 9 pounds. Yearling lamb is tender but has a strong flavor.

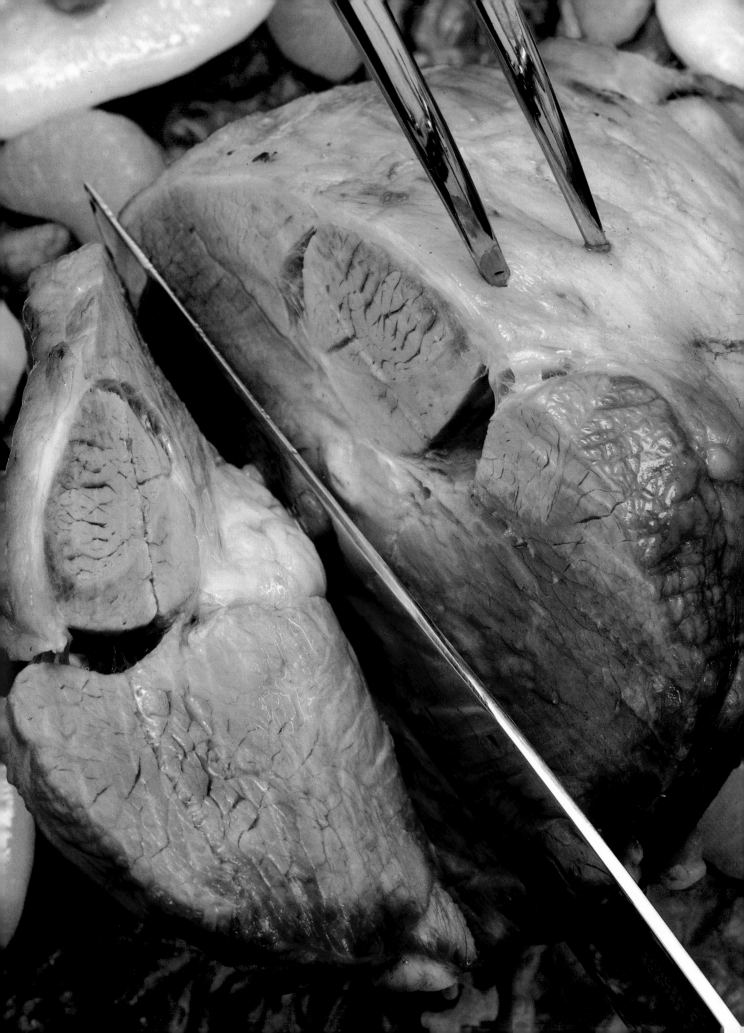

Selecting, Storing & Freezing Lamb

All lamb is tender. The flavor becomes more pronounced as the animal matures. Avoid lamb with coarse-grained lean or soft fat. Store and freeze lamb as directed for beef, page 17. If you plan to marinate chops, place them in the marinade immediately after purchase. It will improve their flavor and help keep them fresh.

Chart at right shows popular retail cuts of lamb and the wholesale cuts from which they are taken. It was adapted for microwaving from information supplied by the National Livestock and Meat Board.

Compare the size of lamb chop marketed in late fall with a "spring" lamb chop. Good lamb of any age has fine, velvety lean and firm, almost waxy fat.

Check your supermarket freezer case for New Zealand lamb. It's a good buy when fresh lamb is scarce.

Lamb Storage Chart

Cut	Refrigerator	Freezer Compartment	Freezer (−0°)
Roasts	3-5 days	No more than 1 week, unless you are sure temperature is below 0°. Defrosting times in this book are based on 0° freezer temperature.	6-7 months
Chops	3-4 days		6-7 months
Stuffed Cushion Shoulder, Breast or Chops	24 hours		3-4 months
Cubed Lamb	2 days		3-4 months
Ground Lamb	24 hours		3-4 months

Lamb Defrosting Chart

Cut	Comments	50% (Medium) Min./Lb.	30% (Low) Min./Lb.
Roasts	Follow directions for roasts over over 2-in. thick, page 20, but let stand 15 to 20 minutes after defrosting.	5-8	8½-13
Rib and Loin Chops	Follow directions for small steaks, page 21; shield tails with foil after half the defrosting time.	4-6½	6¾-10¾
Sirloin Chops (Steaks)	Follow directions for small steaks, page 21, but let stand 15 to 20 minutes after defrosting.	4-7	6¾-11½
Cubes	Follow directions for beef cubes, page 23.	4½-6½	6¾-10¾
Ground Lamb	Follow directions for ground beef, page 22.	3¾-4¾	5-7

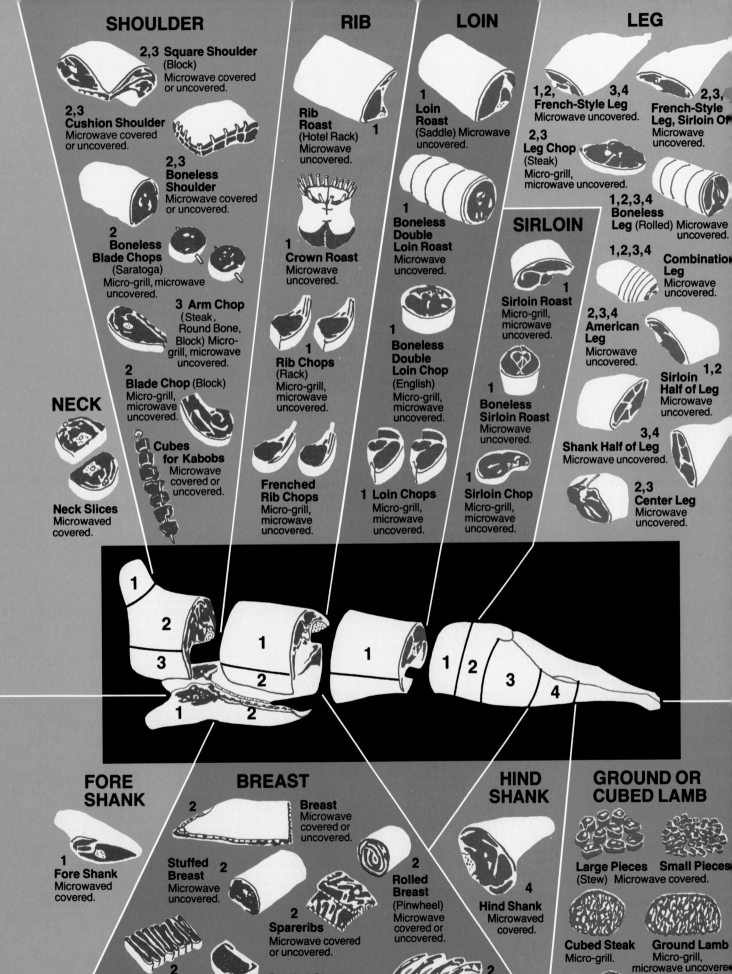

SHOULDER

2,3 Square Shoulder (Block) Microwave covered or uncovered.

2,3 Cushion Shoulder Microwave covered or uncovered.

2,3 Boneless Shoulder Microwave covered or uncovered.

2 Boneless Blade Chops (Saratoga) Micro-grill, microwave uncovered.

3 Arm Chop (Steak, Round Bone, Block) Micro-grill, microwave uncovered.

2 Blade Chop (Block) Micro-grill, microwave uncovered.

Cubes for Kabobs Microwave covered or uncovered.

NECK

Neck Slices Microwaved covered.

RIB

1 Rib Roast (Hotel Rack) Microwave uncovered.

1 Crown Roast Microwave uncovered.

1 Rib Chops (Rack) Micro-grill, microwave uncovered.

Frenched Rib Chops Micro-grill, microwave uncovered.

LOIN

1 Loin Roast (Saddle) Microwave uncovered.

1 Boneless Double Loin Roast Microwave uncovered.

1 Boneless Double Loin Chop (English) Micro-grill, microwave uncovered.

1 Loin Chops Micro-grill, microwave uncovered.

LEG

1,2 French-Style Leg Microwave uncovered.

3,4 French-Style Leg, Sirloin Off Microwave uncovered.

2,3 French-Style Leg, Sirloin Off

2,3 Leg Chop (Steak) Micro-grill, microwave uncovered.

1,2,3,4 Boneless Leg (Rolled) Microwave uncovered.

1,2,3,4 Combination Leg Microwave uncovered.

2,3,4 American Leg Microwave uncovered.

1,2 Sirloin Half of Leg Microwave uncovered.

3,4 Shank Half of Leg Microwave uncovered.

2,3 Center Leg Microwave uncovered.

SIRLOIN

1 Sirloin Roast Micro-grill, microwave uncovered.

1 Boneless Sirloin Roast Microwave uncovered.

1 Sirloin Chop Micro-grill, microwave uncovered.

FORE SHANK

1 Fore Shank Microwaved covered.

BREAST

2 Breast Microwave covered or uncovered.

2 Stuffed Breast Microwave uncovered.

2 Spareribs Microwave covered or uncovered.

2 Rolled Breast (Pinwheel) Microwave covered or uncovered.

2 Stuffed Chops Micro-grill, microwave uncovered.

2 Boneless Riblets Microwave covered.

HIND SHANK

4 Hind Shank Microwaved covered.

2 Riblets Microwave covered.

GROUND OR CUBED LAMB

Large Pieces (Stew) Microwave covered.

Small Pieces

Cubed Steak Micro-grill.

Ground Lamb Micro-grill, microwave uncovered.

Lamb Patties Micro-grill.

Lamb Roasts

Leg of lamb is the most popular lamb roast. A small leg of spring or New Zealand lamb microwaves tender, juicy and nicely browned. With larger, more mature lamb, select the sirloin half or shank half for microwaving. A full leg which is so large that it must be placed in the oven diagonally should be roasted conventionally.

Lamb shoulder also makes a delicious roast. The square-cut shoulder contains a good deal of fat and complicated bones. Boneless, rolled shoulder is easier to cook and carve.

Almost any herb goes well with lamb. Sliver 2 or 3 cloves of peeled garlic and insert them in the meat; then rub the roast with

How to Insert Probe or Thermometer in a Lamb Roast

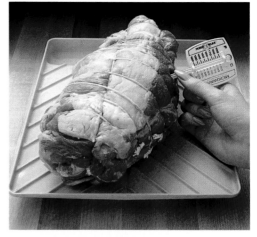

Full Leg. Insert sensor from the side so tip is in center or meaty area below the joint and does not touch bone.

Sirloin or Shank Half. Insert sensor from cut end or side into meatiest area, about ¾-in. away from bone.

Boneless Shoulder. Insert sensor from end or side so tip is in center of meat but not touching fat.

How to Microwave Lamb Roasts

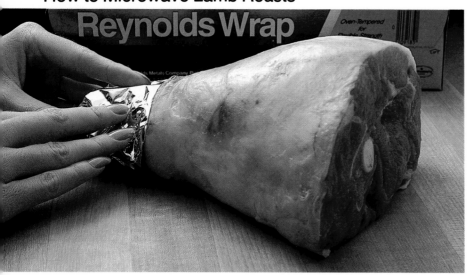

Shield full leg or shank half with foil over end of bone to cover 2 inches of meat. Sirloin half and shoulders need no shielding.

Place roast on rack in baking dish, fat side down. Insert micro-wave thermometer, if used.

rosemary or thyme. Try tarragon, without the garlic, for variety. Lamb needs no tenderizing, but the wine marinade, page 31, or the lemon marinade, page 106, will enhance its flavor.

Full Leg or Sirloin Half

Approx. Total Time: Min/Lb.	Start at High Power	Finish at 50% (Medium)	Remove at Internal Temp.
8-11	First 5 min.	Rare	120°
9-12¾	First 5 min.	Medium	135°
10-14	First 5 min.	Well Done	150°

Shank Half

Approx. Total Time: Min/Lb.	Start at High Power	Finish at 50% (Medium)	Remove at Internal Temp.
4½-6¾	First 5 min.	Rare	120°
6½-8½	First 5 min.	Medium	135°
7-9½	First 5 min.	Well Done	150°

Shoulder

Approx. Total Time: Min/Lb.	Start at High Power	Finish at 50% (Medium)	Remove at Internal Temp.
9-12¾	Under 4 lbs. first 3 min.	Rare	120°
10½-14¼	Over 4 lbs. first 5 min.	Medium	130°
12-15½		Well Done	150°

Square Shoulder. Insert sensor from end with round bone so tip is near center of meatiest area, but not touching bone.

Estimate the total cooking time; divide in half. Microwave at High 3 to 5 minutes, as shown on chart. Reduce power to 50% (Medium). Microwave remaining part of first half of cooking time. Remove any shielding. (Insert probe at this time, if used.)

Turn roast over. Microwave until internal temperature reaches removal point for doneness desired. Let stand 10 minutes, tented with foil.

Lamb Chops

Lamb chops may be cut from the rib, loin, leg or shoulder sections. Leg and arm chops are frequently called "steaks". Blade chops contain a good deal of fat and bone. They cost less per pound, but compare the cost per serving before selecting them.

Lamb chops need no tenderizing, but a lemon or wine marinade adds delicious flavor to micro-grilled chops. Dry the chops with paper towels before placing them on the browning utensil. If you don't marinate the chops, try serving them with Dijon mustard or a spoonful of tarragon butter.

Times below are for chops 1-in. thick, medium-rare to medium. See page 24 for doneness test.

Quantity	1st side Minutes	2nd side Minutes
2	1	½-1½
4	1	1½-2½
8	1½	3½-4½

How to Microwave Lamb Chops on a Browning Dish or Grill

Preheat utensil at High as manufacturer directs. (Use grill for 8 chops.)

Place chops on dish. Microwave first side.

Turn chops over. Microwave second side. Remove chops from dish promptly to avoid over-cooking them.

Mushroom Lamb Chops

2 tablespoons butter or
   margarine
1 tablespoon flour
½ teaspoon ginger
½ teaspoon salt
¼ teaspoon garlic powder
⅛ teaspoon pepper
¼ teaspoon bouquet sauce
8 lamb ribs or loin chops,
   approx. 4-oz. each
8 oz. fresh mushrooms, sliced

Serves 4

Melt butter in 3-qt. casserole at High 30 to 50 seconds. Stir in flour, seasonings and bouquet sauce until smooth. Arrange chops in casserole with meaty portions to outside of dish. Add mushrooms, cover. Microwave at High 5 minutes. Reduce power to 50% (Medium). Microwave 9 to 14 minutes for medium-rare to medium, or until lamb is desired doneness, turning over and rearranging lamb after half the cooking time, so least cooked portions are to outside of dish.

Lamb Steaks & Onions

3 tablespoons butter or
   margarine
1 teaspoon parsley flakes
1 teaspoon marjoram
1 teaspoon rosemary, crushed
1 teaspoon salt
4 lamb leg or arm chops
   (1½ to 2-lbs.)
2 medium onions, thinly sliced

Serves 4

Melt butter in 12×8-in. glass dish at High 45 to 60 seconds. Stir in seasonings. Arrange steaks in dish, turning to coat with butter. Add onions, cover with wax paper. Microwave at High 5 minutes. Reduce power to 50% (Medium). Microwave 11 to 16 minutes for medium, or until lamb is desired doneness, turning over and rearranging steaks after half the time, so least cooked portions are to outside.

Lamb Kabobs ▲

1 lb. lamb cut into 24 1-in. cubes
 Lemon Marinade (below)
½ medium green pepper, cut in
 12 strips (½ × 1½-in.)
1 small onion, cut in 8 wedges
1 medium lemon, cut in 8 wedges
4 wooden skewers

Serves 4

Combine lamb and marinade. Let stand covered at room temperature 3 to 4 hours. Discard marinade.

On each skewer place 1 each green pepper strip, lamb cube, onion wedge, lamb cube, lemon wedge, lamb cube. Repeat sequence. Finish with 1 strip green pepper. Do not pack tightly.

Place kabobs on roasting rack. Cover with wax paper. Microwave at 50% (Medium) 6 minutes. Turn over and rearrange. Microwave 5 to 9 minutes.

Lemon Marinade for Lamb

½ cup lemon juice
½ cup olive oil
2 cloves garlic, crushed
 2 bay leaves
 ½ teaspoon thyme
 ½ teaspoon salt
 ¼ teaspoon pepper

Combine all ingredients in small mixing bowl.

Lamb & Zucchini in ▲ Tomato Sauce

1½ to 2 cups cooked lamb,
 ¾-in. cubes
1 medium zucchini, cut in
 ¾-in. cubes
1 can (8-oz.) tomato sauce
1 can (4-oz.) mushroom
 stems and pieces, drained
1 tablespoon brown sugar
1 bay leaf
½ teaspoon basil
¼ teaspoon salt
 Dash pepper

Serves 4

Combine all ingredients in 2-qt. casserole. Cover. Microwave at High 3 minutes. Reduce power to 50% (Medium). Microwave 8 to 12 minutes, or until zucchini is tender, stirring after half the cooking time.

Serve over rice or noodles.

Lamb Stew

2 tablespoons flour
1½ teaspoons seasoned salt
¼ to ½ teaspoon thyme
1 lb. lamb, cut into ¾-in. cubes
¾ cup water
¼ cup sauterne (or water)
1 teaspoon cider vinegar
1 clove garlic, pressed
1 small eggplant, cut in ¾-in.
 cubes
2 medium onions, cut in
 eighths
2 medium tomatoes, peeled
 and cut in wedges
1 large green pepper, cut in
 1-in. chunks

Serves 4 to 6

Mix flour, salt and thyme in 3-qt. casserole. Add lamb; stir to coat. Blend in water, sauterne, vinegar and garlic. Cover. Microwave at 50% (Medium) 20 minutes. Stir in remaining ingredients. Cover. Microwave 25 to 35 minutes, or until lamb is fork tender and vegetables are cooked, stirring after half the cooking time. Let stand covered 10 minutes.

Serve over steamed rice.

Lamb Pilaf

- 1 cup uncooked long grain rice
- 2 cups water
- 1 tablespoon instant chicken bouillon
- ½ teaspoon salt
- ½ cup chopped onion
- ½ cup chopped green pepper
- 1 clove garlic, minced or pressed
- 1 tablespoon olive oil
- ¼ to ½ teaspoon tarragon leaves
- 1½ to 2 cups cooked lamb, ¾ to 1-in. cubes

Serves 4 to 6

How to Microwave Lamb Pilaf

Combine rice, water, bouillon and salt in 2-qt. casserole; cover. Microwave at High 5 minutes, stir. Re-cover. Reduce power to 50% (Medium). Microwave 10 to 12 minutes. Let stand while preparing vegetables.

Combine onion, green pepper, garlic and oil in 1-qt. measure. Microwave at High 2½ to 5 minutes, or until pepper is tender. Stir in tarragon and lamb.

Fluff rice with fork. Remove half of the rice from casserole and set aside.

Spread lamb mixture over rice in casserole. Top with remaining rice. Cover. Reduce power to 50% (Medium). Microwave 3 to 6 minutes, or until heated through.

Liver

Calf, beef and pork liver have similar nutritional value, and can be used interchangeably in these recipes. Calves' liver is more tender and has a milder flavor, but it is expensive.

How to Defrost Liver

50% (Medium) 5-7 min. per lb.
30% (Low) 8½-11 min. per lb.

Place package in oven. Defrost for ⅓ the total time. Turn package over.

Defrost for ⅓ of time. Unwrap and separate pieces. Spread out in baking dish.

Defrost remaining time. Let stand 5 minutes, or until pieces can be pierced with a fork.

How to Defrost Chicken Livers

50% (Medium) 4-6 min. per lb.
30% (Low) 7-9½ min. per lb.

Place package in oven. Defrost for half the total time. Unwrap and separate livers.

Remove any defrosted livers. Spread out the rest in baking dish. Defrost remaining time.

Let stand 5 minutes, or until livers can be pierced with a fork.

Chicken Livers in Browning Dish

1 lb. chicken livers
2 tablespoons butter or
    margarine
½ cup chopped green onion
1 teaspoon salt
    Dash pepper

Serves 4

Preheat browning dish according to manufacturers directions.

Add livers and butter. Microwave at High 1 minute.

Stir in remaining ingredients. Microwave 4½ to 7 minutes, or until livers lose their pink color, stirring after half the cooking time.

Oriental Liver

6 slices bacon, cut in eighths
⅓ cup brown sugar
⅓ cup cider vinegar*
1 tablespoon cornstarch
1 teaspoon salt
¼ teaspoon marjoram
⅛ teaspoon pepper
1 lb. pork or beef liver, cut into
    serving size pieces
1 small onion, chopped
½ medium green pepper,
    chopped

* For sweeter sauce, use ¼ cup
    vinegar

Serves 4

Place bacon in 12×8-in. dish. Cover with wax paper. Microwave at High 5 to 6 minutes. Drain fat from dish.

Stir in brown sugar, vinegar, cornstarch and seasonings. Arrange liver in dish, turning over to coat with sauce. Top with onion and green pepper. Cover with wax paper.

Microwave at High 5 minutes. Reduce power to 50% (Medium). Microwave 12 to 16 minutes, or until liver is fork tender, turning over and rearranging liver after half the cooking time.

Liver, Bacon & Onions ▲

4 slices bacon, cut in sixths
¼ cup flour
1½ teaspoons seasoned salt
1 lb. liver, cut in serving size
    pieces
2 medium onions, thinly sliced
½ cup water

Serves 4

Place bacon in 12×8-in. dish. Cover with plastic wrap. Microwave at High 4 minutes.

While microwaving bacon, combine flour and seasoned salt. Dredge liver in flour. Sprinkle excess flour over pieces. Set aside.

Drain all but 2 tablespoons bacon fat from dish. Place liver in dish. Add remaining ingredients. Cover with plastic wrap. Microwave at High 5 minutes. Reduce power to 50% (Medium). Microwave 11 to 15 minutes, or until liver is fork tender. Turn over and rearrange pieces after half the cooking time.

Liver in Wine Sauce

1 lb. liver, cut in serving size
    pieces
3 tablespoons flour
2 tablespoons butter or
    margarine
1 can (4-oz.) mushroom stems
    and pieces, drained
⅓ cup white wine
1 clove garlic, pressed or
    minced
2 teaspoons parsley flakes
1 teaspoon instant beef bouillon
1 teaspoon salt
    Dash pepper

Serves 4

Preheat browning dish according to manufacturer's directions. While preheating dish, dredge liver in flour.

Place liver and butter in dish. Microwave at High 1½ minutes. Turn liver over; microwave 1½ minutes.

Add remaining ingredients. Reduce power to 50% (Medium). Microwave 11 to 15 minutes, or until liver is fork tender, turning over and rearranging pieces after half the cooking time.

Sausage

Sausage comes in a variety of forms and flavors. Nearly every region or nationality has its specialty. Serve sausage for a hearty main dish as well as for breakfast or lunch.

Fresh pork sausage in bulk or link form and country-style sausage must be thoroughly cooked before serving. Wieners, frankfurters, knockwurst and bologna are fully cooked, but heating improves their flavor. Bratwurst, Polish and other specialty sausages may be either fully cooked or uncooked; ask your butcher. If the sausage is uncooked, microwave it in ½-in. of water until the meat feels firm. Drain and proceed as directed for fully cooked sausage.

◄ Bratwurst & Beer, page 115

Medium Sausages *(Fully Cooked) High Power	
1 sausage	½-¾ min.
2 sausages	¾-1¼ min.
4 sausages	1¾-2¾ min.
Large Sausages (Fully Cooked) High Power	
1 sausage	¾-1¼ min.
2 sausages	1¼-1¾ min.
4 sausages	2-3 min.

*To microwave sausages in buns add 2 to 3 seconds per sausage.

How to Microwave Medium Fully Cooked Sausages

Arrange sausages on plate and cover with wax paper, or place in buns and wrap in paper towels. Microwave according to chart.

Rearrange wieners or other medium-size sausages when heating 4, by bringing outside ones to center.

How to Microwave Large Fully Cooked Sausages

Puncture each sausage twice with a fork. Arrange on plate without buns; cover with wax paper.

Microwave according to chart, turning over and rearranging sausages after half the cooking time.

111

Sausage Storage Chart

Cut	Refrigerator	Freezer Compartment	Freezer (-0°) or below
Fresh bulk and link pork sausage	1-2 days	No more than 1 week, unless you are sure temperature is below 0°. Defrosting times in this book are based on 0° freezer temperature.	1 month
Brown 'n serve	1 week		2 months
Fully cooked sausages	1 week		2 months
Uncooked sausages	1-2 days		1 month

How to Microwave Sausage Patties or Links

Browning Dish Method. Preheat dish as manufacturer directs. Place sausage in dish; microwave first side. Turn over. Microwave second side.

Rack Method. Arrange sausage on rack in baking dish. Combine equal parts bouquet sauce and water. Brush on meat. Cover dish with wax paper. Microwave first side. Turn sausage over, brush with browning mixture. Microwave second side.

Sausage Cooking Chart

High Power

Patties, 2-oz., 3-in. diameter			Sausage Links			Brown & Serve Links		
Quantity	1st side Minutes	2nd side Minutes	Quantity	1st side Minutes	2nd side Minutes	Quantity	1st side Minutes	2nd side Minutes
Rack Method			Rack Method			Rack Method		
2	1-1½	2-2½	2	1	1-1½	2	½	½-1
4	1½-2	2½-3	4	1	1-1½	4	½	1
8	3-3½	4-4½	8	1½-2	2	8	1	1
Browning Dish			Browning Dish			Browning Dish		
2	½	1	2	½	½-1	2	¼	¼-½
4	1½	1½-2	4	½-1	1	4	½	½
8	2	2½-3	8	1-1½	1½	8	½	½-¾

Sausage and Rice

1 lb. fresh sausage links, cut in
   1-in. pieces
½ teaspoon bouquet sauce
½ cup chopped celery
½ cup chopped onion
½ cup chopped green pepper
2 cups cooked rice
2 teaspoons soy sauce
1 teaspoon instant beef bouillon
¼ teaspoon salt

Serves 4

Coat sausage with bouquet sauce. Place in 2-qt. casserole. Cover with wax paper. Microwave at High 5 to 6½ minutes, or until sausage loses its pink color. Separate sausage pieces. Remove to paper towels. Discard fat.

Combine vegetables in casserole; cover with wax paper. Microwave at High 4 to 5½ minutes, or until vegetables are tender.

Stir in sausage and remaining ingredients. Cover with wax paper.

Microwave at High 3 to 5 minutes, or until heated through, stirring after half the cooking time.

Sausage & Corn Custard

8 oz. brown and serve
   sausages, cut in ¾-in.
   pieces
¼ cup finely chopped onion
2 tablespoons flour
1 teaspoon salt
¼ teaspoon dry mustard
⅛ teaspoon pepper
½ cup milk
1 egg, slightly beaten
1 can (16-oz.) whole kernel
   corn, drained

Serves 4

Place sausages and onion in 1½-qt. casserole. Microwave at High 2 to 3 minutes, or until onion is translucent.

Stir in flour and seasonings. Add milk, egg and corn. Cover tightly. Reduce power to 50% (Medium). Microwave 14 to 18 minutes, or until set, rotating after half the cooking time. Let stand 2 to 3 minutes before serving.

Sausage Stuffed Eggplant ▲

¾ lb. bulk pork sausage
1 medium eggplant
½ cup chopped onion
1 can (4-oz.) mushroom stems
   and pieces, drained
¼ cup dry bread crumbs
1 teaspoon Worcestershire
   sauce

½ teaspoon seasoned salt
¼ teaspoon basil
¼ cup water
¾ cup shredded cheddar
   cheese

Serves 4

Break up sausage in 2-qt. casserole. Cover. Microwave at High 3½ to 5 minutes, or until sausage loses its pink color. While microwaving sausage, cut eggplant in half. Scoop out pulp, leaving ¼-in. shell. Chop pulp coarsely. Break up sausage and drain on paper towels. Discard fat.

Combine chopped eggplant and onion in casserole. Microwave at High 3 to 4 minutes, or until onion is translucent. Stir in sausage, mushrooms, bread crumbs, Worcestershire sauce and seasonings.

Spoon half of sausage mixture into each eggplant shell. Pour water into 8×8-in. glass dish. Set eggplant halves in dish; cover. Microwave at High 5 to 6 minutes, or until eggplant is fork tender.

Sprinkle cheese over eggplant. Reduce power to 50% (Medium). Microwave 1½ to 2 minutes, uncovered, or until cheese melts.

Bologna & Scalloped Potatoes

    3 tablespoons butter
    3 tablespoons flour
    1 teaspoon parsley flakes
    ½ teaspoon salt
    ⅛ teaspoon pepper
1½ cups milk
    3 medium potatoes peeled
        and thinly sliced (3 cups)
    1 ring bologna, skinned and
        cut in 2-in. pieces

Serves 4

Melt butter in 2-qt. casserole at High, 40 to 60 seconds. Stir in flour, parsley flakes and seasonings until smooth. Blend in milk. Microwave at High 5 to 7 minutes or until thickened, stirring twice during cooking.

Mix in potatoes. Cover tightly. Microwave at High 8 to 9 minutes, or until potatoes are almost fork tender. Stir.

Place bologna pieces on top of potatoes. Cover. Microwave at High 4 to 6 minutes or until potatoes are tender and bologna is heated through.

Sausage & Apples

1 tablespoon brown sugar
1 teaspoon flour
3 medium cooking apples, thinly
    sliced
4 individual polish sausages
    (approx. 1-lb.)

Serves 4

Combine brown sugar and flour in 2-qt. casserole. Add apples and toss to coat. Arrange sausages around outer edge of dish. Cover with wax paper. Microwave at High 4 to 8 minutes, or until apples are tender and sausages are heated through, stirring apples and rearranging sausage after half the cooking time.

Easy Kraut and Sausage

1½ lbs. bulk pork sausage
  ½ teaspoon bouquet sauce
    (optional)
  1 large onion, chopped
  1 medium apple, chopped
  1 medium carrot, chopped
  1 can (16-oz.) sauerkraut,
    drained
  2 tablespoons brown sugar
  1 tablespoon parsley flakes
  2 teaspoons instant chicken
    bouillon
  ⅛ teaspoon garlic powder

Serves 4 to 6

Crumble sausage into 2-qt. casserole. Microwave at High 6 to 8 minutes, or until sausage has lost pink color. Break up sausage. If browner sausage is desired, stir in bouquet sauce. Drain sausage on paper towels. Discard fat.

Combine onion, apple, and carrot in casserole. Cover tightly. Microwave at High 4 to 6 minutes, or until carrots are tender. Mix in sausage and remaining ingredients. Microwave, uncovered, at High 4 to 6 minutes, or until heated through.

Bratwurst & Beer

2 large onions, thinly sliced,
  separated into rings
1 can (12-oz.) beer, room
  temperature
1 tablespoon butter or
  margarine
1 lb. fully cooked bratwurst

Serves 4 to 6

In 12×8-in. dish, combine onions, beer and butter. Cover with plastic wrap. Microwave at High 4 to 5 minutes or until onions are translucent. Add bratwurst. Cover. Microwave at High 4 to 6 minutes, or until bratwurst is heated through, rearranging after half the cooking time.

Chili & Cheese Dogs ▶

6 wieners
1 can (7½-oz.) chili without
  beans
¼ cup finely chopped onion
3 oz. thinly sliced American
  cheese

Serves 4 to 6

Score wieners diagonally at 1-in. intervals. Place in 1-qt. casserole. Add chili and onions. Cover with wax paper. Microwave at High 3 to 5 minutes, or until hot and bubbly, rearranging wieners after half the cooking time. Place cheese slices on top of wieners. Reduce power to 50% (Medium). Microwave, uncovered, 2½ to 4½ minutes, or until cheese melts. Serve in wiener buns if desired.

115

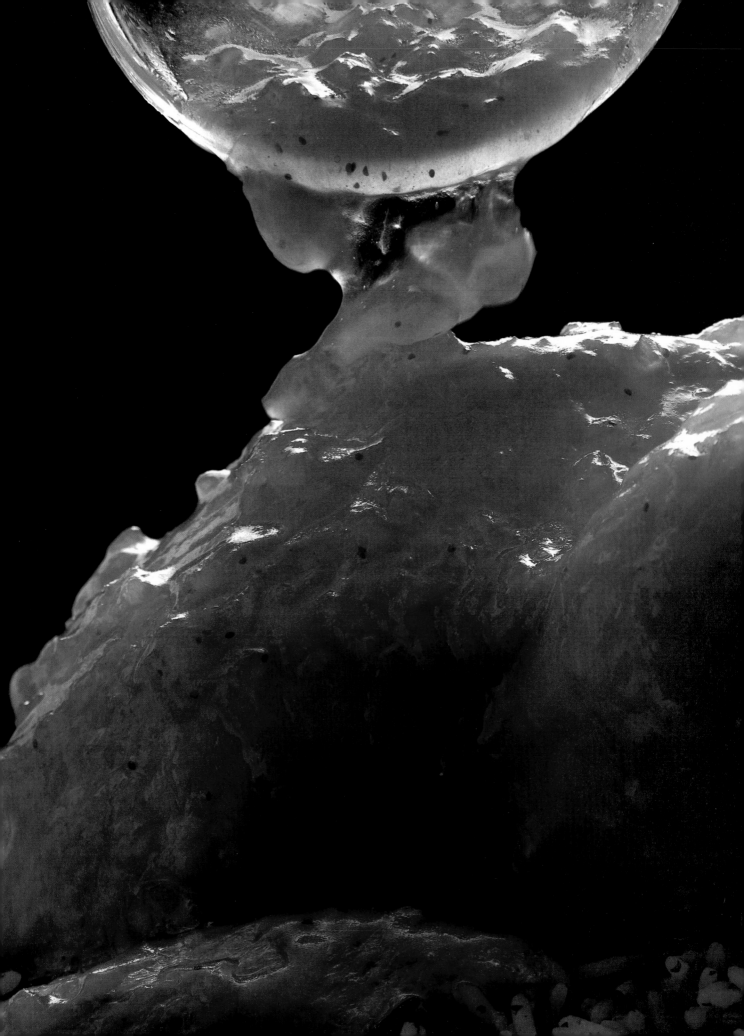

Poultry

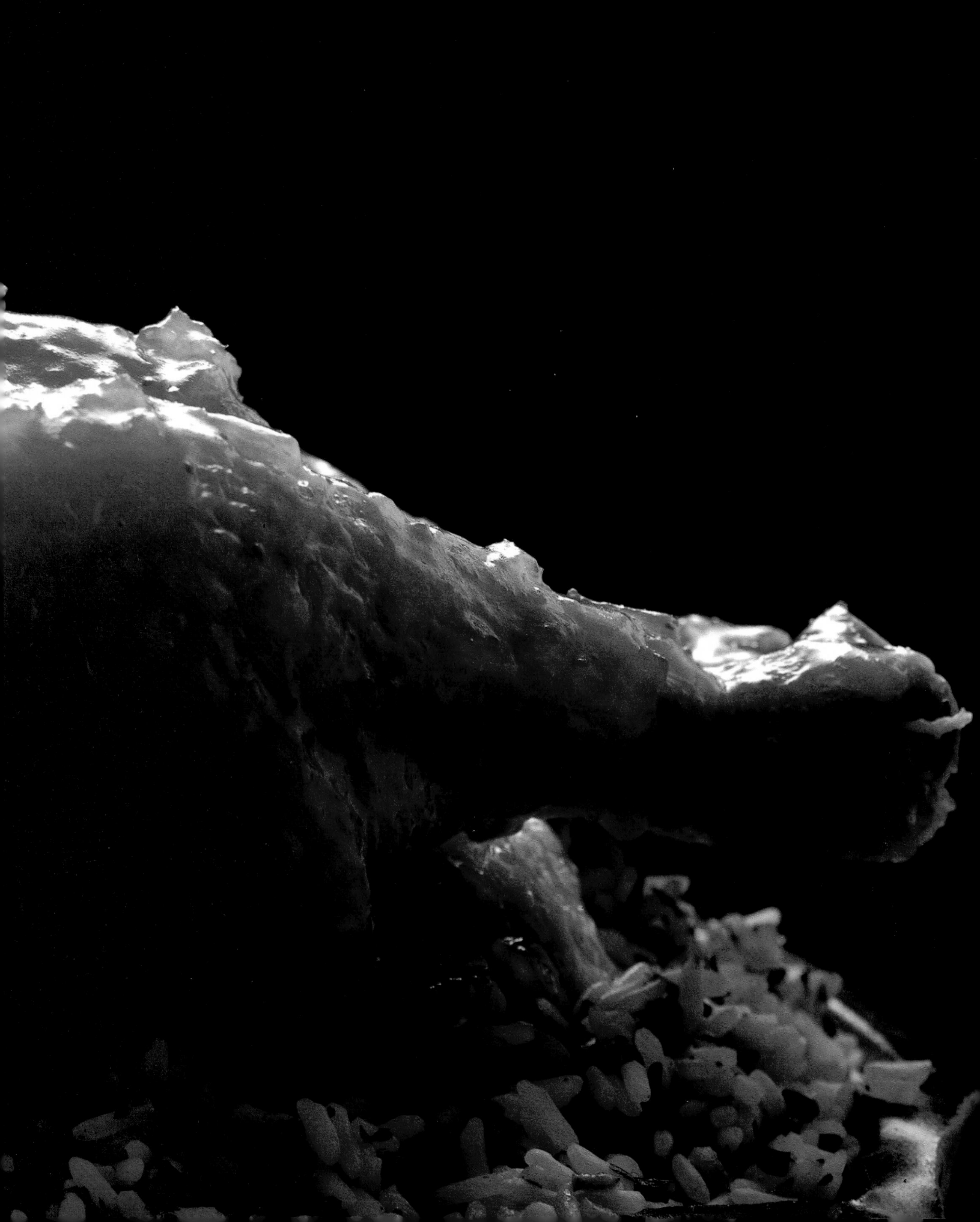

Selecting and Storing Poultry

Chickens are the most common form of fresh poultry, although turkeys and turkey parts are available in some areas. Many supermarkets buy frozen chickens and defrost them for sale. If you plan to freeze this type of chicken, ask for one which is still partially frozen. Chicken is very perishable. Use it the day you buy it, or the next day. Wash chicken well before cooking to remove bacteria and excess fat in skin. Occasionally a chicken will be so oily that a bouquet sauce mixture will not adhere to the skin. Scrub the chicken well with a vegetable brush and hot water to remove the oily film so the mixture will not streak.

How to Select Poultry

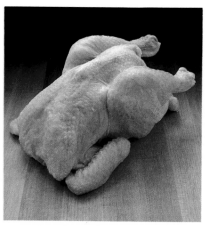

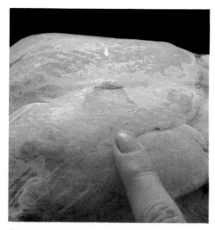

Choose plump broiler-fryers with light-colored, smooth skin, weighing 2½-lbs. or more. Smaller chickens are a poor buy.

Avoid stewing hens, their skin does not tenderize. Fryers with thick yellow skin and large pores are also a poor choice.

Check frozen poultry for tears in packages; they cause freezer burn. Choose fresh chickens with little moisture in package.

How to Brown Poultry

Plain microwaved chicken pieces have a light golden color which many people find acceptable. Whole chicken and turkey develop more browning.

Mix equal parts of bouquet sauce and melted butter. Rub into well-dried chicken skin. Butter helps keep the liquid from beading up on the fatty surface. Dilute bouquet sauce with water for Cornish hens which are not fatty.

How Much Poultry to Buy

The number of people a bird will serve depends on the proportion of meat to bone. The general rule is ¾ to 1-lb. per serving of poultry under 12-lbs., and ½ to ¾-lb. per serving if it is over 12-lbs. Use this as a guide when buying poultry parts, roasting chickens and turkeys.

Some people like to microwave a whole turkey or a turkey breast, then cube the meat for a salad or casserole to serve a crowd. In this case, you will need less meat per serving because it is mixed with other ingredients, but allow for second helpings.

A 1½-lb. broiler-fryer serves 2; a 2½-lb. fryer has a better ratio of

meat to bone and serves 4. If your family is small, the larger fryer may still be a better buy. You can freeze part of it, or microwave it all and use some for sandwiches or a casserole.

Ducklings are very bony. A 4 to 5½-lb. bird makes 4 servings. When serving Cornish Hen, buy one per person.

How to Store and Freeze Chicken

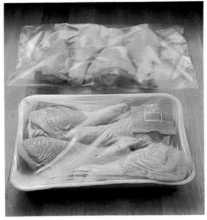

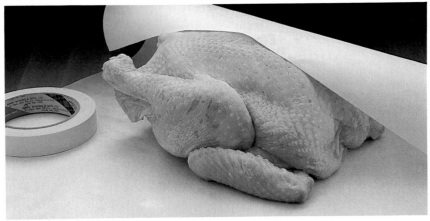

Store chicken in package; use promptly. To keep 2 days, wash in salted water and wrap in plastic wrap or clean, dry plastic bag.

Freeze chicken in original package if you plan to use it within 2 weeks. For longer storage, remove packaging and wrap chicken in wax-coated freezer paper, as directed for beef, page 17.

Brush chicken pieces with melted butter, sprinkle with paprika for warm color and intriguing taste.

Rub chicken or Cornish hens with soy or teriyaki sauce for light color and mild Oriental flavor. Marinate 15 minutes for stronger color and flavor.

Use coatings to give chicken pieces eye and appetite appeal. Try the recipes on page 142.

Defrosting Turkey & Turkey Parts

Defrosting turkey is one of the most appreciated benefits of a microwave oven. You defrost it the day you want it, instead of crowding the refrigerator for 2 or 3 days, and microwave defrosting is safer than defrosting at room temperature.

Turkey Defrosting Chart

Cut	50% (Medium)	30% (Low)
Whole & Half Turkeys	3½-5½ min. per lb.	5½-8 min. per lb.
Turkey Parts	3-6 min. per lb.	7-9½ min. per lb.
Turkey Cutlets	5½-7½ min. per lb.	9½-12½ min. per lb.

How to Defrost Turkey Breasts & Half Turkeys

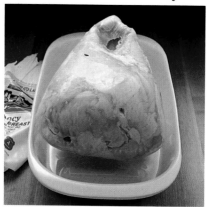

Unwrap turkey; place on rack in baking dish, breast side down. Defrost for half the time.

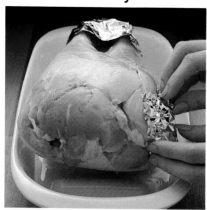

Shield warm or brown spots. Turn breast side up. Defrost remaining time and rinse in cool water.

Let Stand 5 to 10 minutes, or until breast is completely defrosted in area behind wings and cavity is no longer icy.

How to Defrost Whole Turkey

Unwrap turkey so you can feel warm spots as it defrosts. Place breast side down in baking dish. Defrost for ¼ the total time.

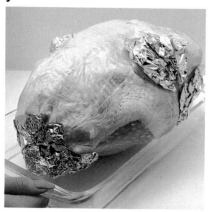

Use foil to shield areas which feel warm, then turn turkey breast side up. Defrost for ¼ the time.

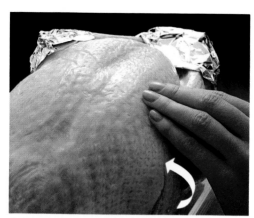

Check for warm or brown spots, shielding them and the leg and wing tips. Turn turkey over.

How to Defrost Turkey Hind Quarters & Legs

Arrange parts on rack in baking dish with meaty areas to outside of dish. Defrost for half the time.

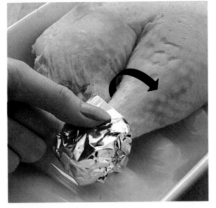

Shield leg tips and warm areas. Turn over and separate pieces. Defrost remaining time until surface is soft but not hot.

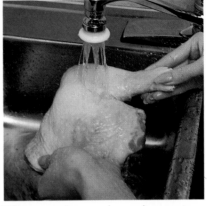

Rinse under cool running water. Let stand 5 minutes, or until thickest part of meat can be pierced to the bone with a fork.

How to Defrost Turkey Cutlets

Place unopened package in oven. Defrost for ⅓ the total time. Turn package over. Defrost for ⅓ of time.

Separate cutlets. Arrange in a single layer on large plate, removing any which are defrosted.

Defrost remaining time, or until cutlets are pliable. Let stand 5 minutes.

Rotate dish. Turkey legs should point to opposite side of oven. Defrost for ¼ the time.

Turn turkey over and defrost remaining time. Spread legs and wings from body; loosen giblets. Place turkey in cool water.

Let Stand 20 to 30 minutes, until giblets and neck can be removed, and cavity is cool but not icy. Make sure breast is defrosted in areas under wings.

Defrosting Poultry

Poultry Defrosting Chart

	50% (Medium)	30% (Low)
Whole Chicken	3-5½ min. per lb.	5-9 min. per lb.
Duckling	4½-6 min. per lb.	7½-10 min. per lb.
Cornish Hens	5-7 min. per lb.	8½-11½ min. per lb.

How to Defrost Whole Chicken, Duckling & Cornish Hens

Unwrap duckling and cornish hens. Leave chicken in paper or plastic package with twist ties removed.

Place bird in baking dish, breast side down. Cover duckling and cornish hens with wax paper. Defrost for half the time.

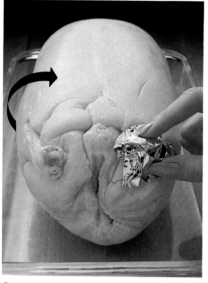

Shield warm spots and leg tips with foil. Turn breast side up. Rearrange cornish hens.

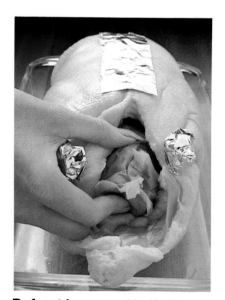

Defrost for second half of time. Spread legs and wings from body; loosen giblets and neck.

Place duckling in bowl of cool water 5 to 10 minutes, or until giblets and neck can be removed.

Let chicken and cornish hens stand 5 minutes. Remove giblets; rinse cavity with cool water until no longer icy.

Poultry Defrosting Chart

	50% (Medium)	30% (Low)
Chicken Quarters	4½-5½ min. per lb.	5½-9 min. per lb.
Chicken Pieces	2½-5 min. per lb.	4½-8½ min. per lb.
Boneless Chicken Breasts	5½-8 min. per lb.	9-13 min. per lb.

How to Defrost Chicken Quarters and Pieces

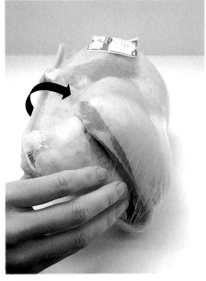

Place paper or plastic-wrapped package in oven. Defrost for half the total time. Turn package over. Defrost for ¼ the total time.

Unwrap and separate pieces. Arrange in baking dish with meatiest parts to outside. Defrost remaining time.

Let stand 5 minutes, or until pieces feel soft but still cold. Wash before using.

How to Defrost Boneless Chicken Breasts

Place paper or plastic-wrapped package in oven. Defrost for half the total time.

Unwrap and separate pieces. Arrange on rack with least defrosted parts to outside.

Defrost for remaining time, or until pieces feel soft but cold.

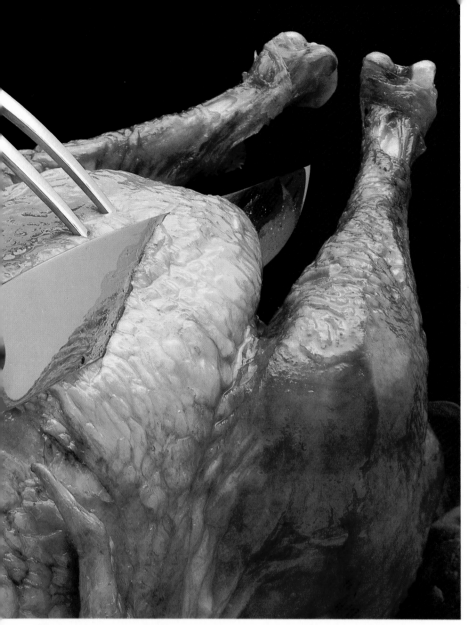

Turkey

The maximum size for a microwaved turkey is 12 to 14 pounds. Larger birds should be roasted conventionally. If you have a small oven, test the cavity size before microwaving. Place turkey in oven and turn it on all sides. There should be 3-in. of space between turkey and oven walls, and at least 2-in. between the top of the oven and the upper side of the turkey.

During microwaving, baste the turkey occasionally and check through the oven door for areas which are browning too fast. Shield these as they occur and leave the shields on when you turn the turkey.

Microwaving times are the same whether the turkey is stuffed or unstuffed. Do not use a temperature probe when microwaving turkey. Hot fat can run down the probe and turn the oven off before the turkey is done. If you check temperature with a thermometer, allow 1 minute for an accurate reading. Since bone reflects some microwave energy, the breast area beneath the wing may be done last.

Turkey microwaves juicy and tender; the skin turns brown.

How to Microwave Whole Turkey   50% (Medium) 12-15 min. per lb.

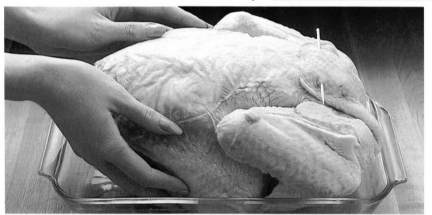

Place turkey, breast side down, in baking dish. Estimate the total cooking time; divide in quarters. Microwave at High first 10 minutes. Reduce power to 50% (Medium). Microwave remaining part of first ¼ of time, checking occasionally and shielding as needed.

Turn turkey on its side. Microwave ¼ of time. Turn other side up. Microwave ¼ of time. (Baste and shield turkey as needed.)

How to Microwave Frozen Turkey Roast

1-2 lbs. 50% (Medium) 23½-28½ min. per lb. (Over 2 lbs. cook conventionally)

Remove frozen loaf to glass loaf dish. Cover with wax paper. Estimate the total cooking time; divide in half.

Microwave at High first 5 minutes. Reduce power to 50% (Medium). Microwave remaining part of first half of time.

Rotate dish. Microwave second half of time, or until internal temperature reaches 175°. Let stand 5 minutes.

How to Microwave Turkey Breast 50% (Medium) 10½-15 min. per lb.

Place breast side down in baking dish. Estimate the total cooking time; divide in half. Microwave at High first five minutes.

Reduce power to 50% (Medium). Microwave remaining part of first half of time. Turn breast side up. Glaze with jelly, if desired.

Microwave remaining time, or until temperature of meatiest area reaches 170°. Let stand 10 to 20 minutes, tented with foil.

Turn breast side up. Microwave ¼ of time, or until turkey is done (shown at right). Let stand 20 to 30 minutes, tented with foil.

Leg moves freely at joint and flesh feels very soft when pressed. Internal temperature of meatiest part of thigh registers 185° after 1 minute. Juices run clear yellow when breast meat under wing is pierced with a skewer.

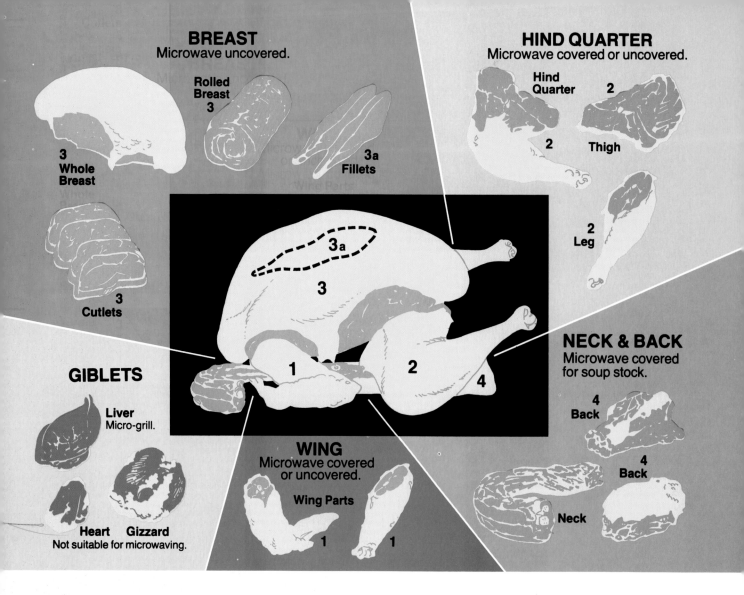

BREAST
Microwave uncovered.

3 Whole Breast

Rolled Breast 3

3a Fillets

3 Cutlets

HIND QUARTER
Microwave covered or uncovered.

Hind Quarter

2

2

2 Thigh

2 Leg

GIBLETS

Liver Micro-grill.

Heart **Gizzard**
Not suitable for microwaving.

NECK & BACK
Microwave covered for soup stock.

4 Back

4 Back

Neck

WING
Microwave covered or uncovered.

Wing Parts

1 **1**

How to Make Cutlets from Turkey Breast

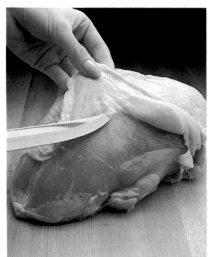

Chill meat thoroughly. Skin turkey breast. Carve one side at a time as you would for serving.

Hold knife parallel to ribs, about 45° angle to cutting board.

Carve large, ¼-in. thick slices. There will be some small pieces; use them for turkey strips.

126

Turkey chart shows how to cut up fresh turkeys when they are available. Freeze the parts in family-size packages. To cut up turkey, cut into shoulder socket and remove wing (1). Remove hind quarter (2) at hip joint. Separate breast (3) from back by cutting through cavity tissue and rib cartilage. Use breast as a roast or slice into cutlets. You may also make cutlets from frozen turkey breasts. Carve the partially defrosted breast in ¼-in. slices as you would for serving. You may refreeze the cutlets as long as ice crystals remain in the meat.

How to Microwave a Half Turkey or Turkey Hind Quarter

50% (Medium) 13-16 min. per lb.

Place turkey on rack, cut side up. Cover with wax paper. Estimate the total cooking time; divide in half. Microwave at High first 10 minutes. Reduce power to 50% (Medium).

Microwave remaining part of first half of time. Turn turkey over. Brush skin evenly with mixture of ½ teaspoon each melted butter and bouquet sauce. Re-cover.

Microwave remaining time, or until internal temperature of inside thigh muscle registers 185° in thickest part. Let stand 10 minutes, tented with foil.

How to Microwave Turkey Legs or Thighs

High first 3 min., 2 pieces
High first 5 min., 4 pieces
50% (Medium) 12-16 min. per lb.

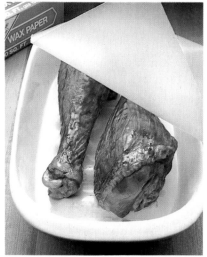

Arrange turkey pieces on rack with meatiest parts to outside. Combine 2 tablespoons each melted butter and bouquet sauce. Brush meat with half of mixture.

Cover with wax paper. Estimate total cooking time; divide in half. Microwave at High as directed in time box. Reduce power to 50% (Medium). Microwave remaining part of first half of time.

Turn over and rearrange turkey parts. Brush with remaining sauce. Microwave second half of time, or until meat near bone is no longer pink and juices run clear.

Cranberry-Pineapple Turkey Legs ▲

12-16 min./lb.

1 can (8-oz.) whole cranberry
   sauce
1 can (8¼-oz.) crushed
   pineapple, drained
2 teaspoons finely grated
   orange peel

10 drops red vegetable food
   coloring
4 turkey legs
2 tablespoons butter or
   margarine
2 tablespoons bouquet sauce

Serves 4

In 2-cup measure, combine cranberry sauce, pineapple, orange peel, and food coloring. Set aside.

Place turkey legs on rack with meatiest parts to outside. In custard cup, melt butter at High 30 to 45 seconds. Stir in bouquet sauce. Brush turkey legs with half of butter mixture. Top with half of cranberry mixture. Cover with wax paper.

Microwave at High first 5 minutes. Reduce power to 50% (Medium). Microwave remainder of first half of time. Turn legs over, brush with butter mixture, top with remaining cranberry mixture. Cover. Microwave remaining time, or until meat next to bone loses pink color and juices run clear.

NOTE: For 2 legs, start at High first 3 minutes, proceed as directed. Serve with extra sauce, if desired.

Barbecued Turkey Legs

10-14 min./lb.

1 cup bottled barbecue sauce
2 teaspoons prepared mustard
1 teaspoon lemon juice
4 turkey legs

Serves 4

In 2-cup measure, mix barbecue sauce, mustard and lemon juice. Set aside. Place turkey legs in 8×8-in. or 12×8-in. dish with meatiest parts to outside of dish.

Brush with half the sauce. Cover tightly. Microwave at High first 5 minutes. Reduce power to 50% (Medium). Microwave remainder of first half of time. Turn over and rearrange legs. Coat with remaining sauce. Re-cover. Microwave remaining time, or until meat near bone is no longer pink and juices run clear.

NOTE: For 2 legs, reduce sauce by half. Start at High first 3 minutes, continue as directed.

Glazed Turkey Hind Quarters
13-16 min./lb.

1 cup orange juice
½ cup brown sugar
2 tablespoons cornstarch
2 turkey hindquarters

Serves 4 to 6

In 2-cup measure, combine juice, sugar and cornstarch. Microwave at High 2½ to 5½ minutes, or until thickened, stirring once or twice.

Place turkey parts on roasting rack skin side down. Brush lightly with glaze. Microwave at High first 5 minutes. Reduce power to 50% (Medium). Microwave remainder of first half of time.

Turn turkey skin side up. Brush with glaze. Microwave remaining time, or until meat near bone is no longer pink and juices run clear.

Microwave any remaining glaze at High ½ to 1½ minutes and serve with turkey.

Creamy Turkey Thighs
15¾-19¾ min./lb.

1 can (10¾-oz.) cream of chicken soup
1 teaspoon Worcestershire sauce
1 teaspoon parsley flakes
½ teaspoon poultry seasoning or ¼ teaspoon sage
2 turkey thighs

Serves 4

In 2-cup measure, combine all ingredients except turkey thighs. Place thighs, skin side down, in 8×8-in. dish. Pour sauce over turkey. Cover with wax paper. Microwave at High first 5 minutes. Reduce power to 50% (Medium). Microwave remainder of first half of time.

Turn over and rearrange thighs. Spoon sauce over meat. Cover. Microwave remaining time, or until meat near bone is no longer pink and juices run clear. Skim excess fat.

NOTE: Turkey may be skinned before cooking.

Honey-Glazed▲ Turkey Wings
12½-17 min./lb.

½ cup honey
1 tablespoon grated lemon rind
2 teaspoons lemon juice
¼ teaspoon bouquet sauce
4 turkey wings

Serves 4

Combine all ingredients except turkey wings in 2-cup measure. Microwave at High 1 to 3 minutes.

Place wings meatiest side down on roasting rack, brush with half the glaze. Microwave at High first 5 minutes. Reduce power to 50% (Medium). Microwave remainder of first half of time.

Turn over and rearrange wings. Brush with remaining glaze. Microwave for second half of time or until meat near bone is no longer pink.

129

◄ Turkey Cutlets Divan

1 package (10-oz.) frozen
   chopped broccoli
1 can (10¾-oz.) cream of
   chicken soup
2 tablespoons sherry
½ teaspoon salt
1 lb. turkey cutlets, flattened to
   ¼-in. thickness
¼ cup Parmesan cheese
¼ cup corn flake crumbs
2 teaspoons parsley flakes

Serves 4

Microwave broccoli in package at High 3 to 4 minutes, or until defrosted. Drain well. Combine broccoli, soup, sherry, and salt in 12×8-in. dish. Spread to cover bottom of dish. Top with cutlets in single layer. Cover with wax paper. Microwave at High 3 minutes.

Reduce power to 50% (Medium). Microwave 8 minutes. Turn over and rearrange cutlets. Combine cheese, crumbs and parsley in small mixing bowl. Sprinkle evenly over cutlets. Microwave, uncovered, 7 to 11 minutes, or until turkey is no longer pink.

Stuffed Turkey Cutlets, Italian Style

1 package (9-oz.) frozen French
   style green beans
4 turkey cutlets (3-4 oz. each)
   flattened to ¼-in. thickness
1 can (8-oz.) tomato sauce
½ teaspoon basil
¼ teaspoon oregano
⅛ teaspoon garlic powder
2 tablespoons Parmesan
   cheese

Serves 4

Microwave beans in package at High 3 to 4 minutes, or until warm. Drain.

Place ¼ of the beans in center of each cutlet. Fold ends of cutlet over beans and secure with wooden picks. Arrange rolls in 8×8-in. glass dish, seam side up. In small bowl, combine tomato sauce and seasonings. Pour over cutlets. Cover with wax paper.

Microwave at 50% (Medium) 10 minutes. Turn rolls over. Spoon sauce over cutlets; sprinkle with cheese. Re-cover. Microwave 6 to 10 minutes, or until turkey is no longer pink.

◄ Turkey Cutlets with Mushrooms & Pea Pods

1 package (6-oz.) frozen
   pea pods
1 lb. turkey cutlets, flattened
   to ¼-in. thickness
½ cup water
1 tablespoon cornstarch

1 tablespoon brown sugar
2 teaspoons chicken bouillon
1 teaspoon soy sauce
½ teaspoon salt
2 cups sliced fresh mushrooms
¼ cup slivered almonds

Serves 4

Microwave pea pods in package at High 1 to 2 minutes, or until defrosted. Set aside.

Place cutlets in single layer in 12×8-in. dish. Cover with plastic wrap. Microwave at 50% (Medium) 6½ to 9 minutes, or until turkey loses its pink color, turning over and rearranging cutlets after half the cooking time. Remove cutlets to platter and cover to keep warm.

In custard cup, blend water and cornstarch together. In 12×8-in. dish, combine cornstarch mixture, brown sugar, bouillon, soy sauce, salt and mushrooms. Microwave, uncovered, at High 5½ to 7½ minutes, or until thickened, stirring twice during cooking.

Stir in pea pods and almonds. Arrange cutlets on top, turning them over to coat lightly with sauce. Microwave 2 to 3 minutes, or until heated through.

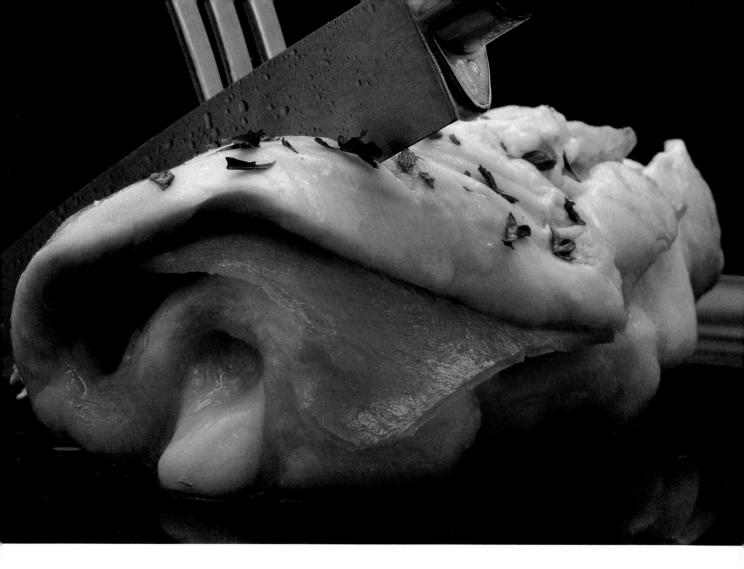

Rolled Turkey, Ham ▲ & Cheese

4 thin slices packaged cooked
    ham
4 thin slices Swiss cheese
4 turkey cutlets (3-4 oz. each)
    flattened to ¼-in. thickness
½ teaspoon parsley flakes or
    1 sprig fresh parsley,
    snipped

Serves 4

Trim ham and cheese to fit cutlets. Place one slice ham and
cheese on each cutlet. Starting
at narrow end, roll up each cutlet
and secure with wooden picks.
Arrange seam side up in 8×8-in.
dish. Cover with wax paper.

Microwave at 50% (Medium) 6
minutes. Turn rolls over. Sprinkle
with parsley. Cover. Microwave
4 to 7 minutes, or until turkey is
no longer pink.

Creamed Turkey with Green Noodles

2 tablespoons butter or
    margarine
2 tablespoons flour
¼ teaspoon salt
⅛ teaspoon pepper
1 cup milk
4 slices bacon, cut in eighths

1 lb. boneless turkey, cut in thin
    strips
1 clove garlic, crushed
½ teaspoon basil
4 oz. shredded Mozarrella
    cheese
Cooked spinach noodles

Serves 4

In 1-qt. measure, melt butter at High 30 to 50 seconds. Stir in flour
and seasonings. Blend in milk. Microwave 6 to 8 minutes, or until
thickened, stirring every minute. Set aside.

Place bacon in 2-qt. casserole; cover. Microwave 3 to 4 minutes, or
until crisp. Drain.

Add turkey, sauce, garlic and basil. Cover. Microwave at 50%
(Medium) 11 to 15 minutes, or until turkey is no longer pink, stirring
twice during cooking. Blend in cheese until smooth. Serve over
spinach noodles.

Whole Chicken

When a whole chicken is microwaved uncovered, it is similar to conventionally roasted. The skin does not crisp but it develops some browning. For more even color, use a browning agent or a glaze. To prevent streaking, scrub off any oily film on the chicken skin with a vegetable brush and hot water before applying the browning mixture.

How to Microwave a Whole Chicken

Wash and dry chicken well. Mix equal parts bouquet sauce and melted butter; rub or brush into skin. (If preferred, glaze chicken after half the cooking time.)

Place chicken breast side down in baking dish. Microwave at High first 3 minutes. Reduce power to 50% (Medium). Microwave remainder of first half of time.

Turn breast side up. (Glaze, if desired.) Microwave second half of time, or until legs move freely and inner thigh meat is done.

◄ Casseroled Chicken   11-13½ min./lb.

1 package (10-oz.) frozen mixed vegetables
2½ to 4-lb. broiler-fryer chicken
1 teaspoon butter or margarine
1 teaspoon bouquet sauce
2 cups (4-oz.) cooked egg noodles
1 can (10¾-oz.) cream of celery soup
¼ cup finely chopped onion
2 tablespoons milk
1 teaspoon instant chicken bouillon
¼ teaspoon dry mustard
¼ teaspoon salt
Dash pepper

Serves 4 to 6

Defrost vegetables in package at High, 2½ to 4½ minutes. Set aside. Place chicken in 3-qt. casserole breast side down. In custard cup, melt butter at High 20 to 45 seconds. Add bouquet sauce.

Brush back of chicken with half of butter mixture. Microwave at High first 3 minutes. Reduce power to 50% (Medium). Microwave remainder of first half of cooking time. While chicken is microwaving, combine remaining ingredients in small bowl.

After half of total time, drain fat from casserole. Turn chicken breast side up, brush with butter sauce mixture. Arrange noodle mixture around the chicken. Microwave remaining time, or until chicken is tender, and legs move freely. Stir noodle mixture before serving.

NOTE: If necessary, skim excess fat from casserole before stirring.

Glazed Chicken   10-13 min./lb.

1 jar (12-oz.) pineapple preserves (1 cup)
¾ cup Russian salad dressing
2½ to 3½-lb. broiler-fryer chicken

Serves 4

In 2-cup measure, combine preserves and dressing.

Place chicken breast side down on roasting rack. Cover with ⅓ of glaze. Microwave at High first 3 minutes. Reduce power to 50% (Medium). Microwave remainder of first half of cooking time.

Turn chicken breast side up, cover with half of remaining glaze. Microwave second half of time, or until leg moves easily and juice runs clear, pouring remaining glaze over chicken during last 5 minutes of cooking.

133

Braised Chicken & Vegetable Dinner

1 teaspoon butter or
   margarine
1 teaspoon bouquet sauce
4 medium carrots, peeled and
   cut in ¼-in. slices
2 medium potatoes, peeled
   and quartered
1 stalk celery, cut in ¼-in.
   slices
1 medium onion, cut in eighths
¼ cup water
1 teaspoon instant chicken
   bouillon
1 bay leaf
½ teaspoon salt
¼ teaspoon pepper
2½ to 3½-lb. broiler-fryer
   chicken

Serves 4 to 6

How to Microwave Braised Chicken & Vegetable Dinner

Melt butter in small dish at High 20 to 40 seconds. Stir in bouquet sauce. Set aside.

Place all ingredients except chicken in large plastic cooking bag; set bag in 12×8-in. baking dish for support.

Brush back of chicken with half of butter mixture. Place chicken in bag breast side down.

Tie end of bag loosely with plastic strip cut from end of bag. Microwave at High 15 minutes.

Open bag carefully. Turn chicken over. Brush breast side with remaining butter mixture. Reseal bag.

Microwave 10 to 15 minutes, or until legs move easily, meat around bone is done and vegetables are tender.

Whole Chicken	
High Power	Finish at 50% (Medium)
first 3 min.	10-13 min./lb.

Vegetable Stuffed Chicken

Stuffing:

1½ cups cubed eggplant, cut in ½ to ¾-in. cubes

1 medium green pepper, cut in ¾-in. chunks

1 medium tomato, peeled, coarsely diced

½ cup chopped onion

1 clove garlic, pressed or minced

1 tablespoon olive oil

½ to 1 teaspoon basil leaves

2 to 3 lb. broiler-fryer chicken

1 tablespoon butter or margarine

1 tablespoon bouquet sauce

Serves 4

In 1-qt. measure combine stuffing ingredients. Microwave at High 4 to 6 minutes, or until vegetables soften. Spoon stuffing into cavity of chicken. Place chicken breast side down on roasting rack.

In custard cup melt butter at High ½ to ¾ minutes. Stir in bouquet sauce. Brush chicken with half the bouquet sauce mixture. Microwave at High first 3 minutes. Reduce power to 50% (Medium). Microwave remainder of first half of cooking time. Turn chicken breast side up. Brush with bouquet sauce mixture. Microwave second half of time, or until legs move freely.

Italian Sauced Chicken

1 can (16-oz.) whole tomatoes

1 envelope (1.5-oz.) spaghetti sauce mix

1 teaspoon Worcestershire sauce

¼ teaspoon crushed tarragon leaves

2½ to 3½-lb. broiler-fryer chicken

Parmesan cheese, optional

¼ cup hot water, optional

Serves 4

In 1-qt. measure combine tomatoes, spaghetti sauce mix, Worcestershire sauce and tarragon.

Place chicken breast side down in 12×8-in. dish, top with tomato mixture. Cover with wax paper. Microwave at High first 3 minutes. Reduce power to 50% (Medium). Microwave remainder of first half of cooking time.

Turn chicken breast side up; baste with sauce. Re-cover. Microwave second half of time, or until legs move easily and juices run clear. Baste and sprinkle with Parmesan cheese before last 5 minutes of cooking time. Remove chicken to platter and serve sauce on the side. For thinner sauce, stir in water.

Chicken Pieces

For these recipes you may use a quartered or cut up broiler-fryer. If one part of the chicken is a family favorite, substitute an equivalent amount of all breasts, thighs or drum sticks. The chicken pieces may be skinned before cooking, if desired.

How to Microwave Saucy Chicken Pieces

Combine sauce and chicken in baking dish or casserole with meatiest portions of chicken to outside of dish.

Cover and microwave as directed for first part of time. Stir sauce and rearrange chicken with least cooked parts to outside of dish.

Microwave remaining time until chicken is tender and meat near bone is no longer pink. Let stand, covered, 5 minutes to blend flavors.

Chicken in Wine Sauce

Sauce:
2 tablespoons butter or margarine
2 tablespoons flour
1 cup dry white wine
1 tablespoon instant chicken bouillon
1 clove garlic, minced or pressed

½ teaspoon salt
⅛ teaspoon pepper
6 drops hot pepper sauce

2 to 3-lbs. broiler-fryer chicken pieces
1 large onion, sliced and separated into rings
½ cup chopped black or green pitted olives

Serves 4 to 6

In 3 to 5-qt. casserole melt butter at High 30 to 45 seconds. Stir in flour. Blend in wine. Add remaining sauce ingredients.

Arrange chicken in casserole bony side up and meatiest portions to outside of dish. Spoon sauce over chicken. Add onions and olives. Cover with wax paper. Microwave at High 10 minutes. Turn over and rearrange chicken, spooning sauce over each piece. Re-cover. Microwave 10 to 15 minutes, or until chicken is fork tender and meat near bone is no longer pink.

Variation:
Substitute red wine for white wine. Add ½ teaspoon bouquet sauce with wine.

Sweet & Sour Chicken

1 cup catsup
¾ cup apricot preserves
¼ cup chopped onion
¼ cup chopped celery
2 tablespoons cider vinegar
1 teaspoon dry mustard
⅛ teaspoon garlic powder
2 to 3-lbs. broiler-fryer chicken pieces

Serves 4

In 1-qt. measure, combine all ingredients except chicken. Microwave at High 3 to 4 minutes, or until sauce is hot and bubbly. Stir and set aside.

In 12×8-in. dish arrange chicken, bony side up and meatiest portions to outside of dish. Cover with wax paper. Microwave 8 minutes. Drain. Turn and rearrange chicken. Pour sauce over chicken. Cover with wax paper. Microwave 7 to 12 minutes, or until chicken is fork tender and meat next to bone is no longer pink. Serve with sauce.

Chicken in Cream Gravy

This dish is finished at 50% (Medium) because cream is sensitive to high temperatures.

½ cup water
½ cup whipping cream
3 tablespoons cornstarch
1 medium onion, thinly sliced and separated into rings
1 stalk celery, sliced
1 bay leaf
1 teaspoon parsley flakes
1 teaspoon salt
¼ teaspoon marjoram
⅛ teaspoon pepper
2 to 3-lbs. broiler-fryer chicken pieces

Serves 4

Blend water, cream and corn-starch in 3-qt. casserole. Mix in remaining ingredients, except chicken. Add chicken and coat with sauce. Cover. Microwave at High 5 minutes. Reduce power to 50% (Medium). Microwave 18 to 23 minutes, or until chicken loses its pink color, stirring sauce and rearranging chicken after half the cooking time. Stir well and let stand 5 minutes before serving.

Coq Au Vin

4 slices bacon, cut into eighths
⅓ cup flour
½ cup dry red wine
½ cup water
2 tablespoons brandy
2 teaspoons parsley flakes
1 teaspoon instant chicken bouillon
1 teaspoon salt
1 clove garlic, pressed or minced
1 bay leaf
¼ teaspoon thyme
¼ teaspoon pepper
¼ teaspoon bouquet sauce
8 oz. fresh mushrooms, sliced
1 large onion, thinly sliced and separated into rings
2½ to 3¼ lbs. broiler-fryer chicken pieces

Serves 4 to 6

Place bacon in 3-qt. casserole. Cover. Microwave at High 3 to 4 minutes, or until crisp. Drain all but 1 tablespoon fat. Blend in flour. Stir in liquid and season-ings. Add mushrooms, onion and chicken. Cover.

Microwave at High 15 minutes. Stir sauce and rearrange chick-en. Microwave, uncovered, 8 to 11 minutes, or until chicken is fork tender. Let stand, covered, 5 minutes before serving.

Chicken Cacciatore ▲

½ cup dry white wine
1 can (16-oz.) whole tomatoes
1 can (6-oz.) tomato paste
1 clove garlic, pressed or minced
1 large bay leaf
1 teaspoon crushed oregano or basil leaves
½ teaspoon salt
¼ teaspoon ground thyme
2 to 3-lbs. broiler-fryer chicken pieces
1 large onion, sliced and separated into rings

Serves 4 to 6

In 1-qt. measure, combine wine, tomatoes, tomato paste and seasonings. Set aside.

In 3 to 5-qt. casserole arrange chicken pieces bony side up and meatiest portions to outside of dish. Add onion rings and top with tomato mixture. Cover tightly. Microwave at High 15 minutes. Turn and rearrange chicken. Microwave 10 to 15 minutes, or until chicken is fork tender and no longer pink. Let stand, covered, 5 minutes. Serve with rice if desired.

Stuffed Chicken Thighs

¼ cup chopped onion
¼ cup chopped celery
2 tablespoons butter or margarine
1 cup herb seasoned stuffing mix
⅓ cup hot water
4 chicken thighs
1 tablespoon melted butter or margarine mixed with 1 tablespoon bouquet sauce optional

Serves 4

Creamy Chicken & Rice

1 can (10¾-oz.) cream of chicken soup
2 cups quick-cooking rice
½ cup water
1 can (4-oz.) mushroom stems and pieces, drained
1 envelope dry onion soup mix
2 to 3-lbs. broiler-fryer chicken pieces

Serves 4

Combine all ingredients, except chicken, in 12×8-in. dish. Arrange chicken pieces on top, bony side up and meatiest parts to outside of dish. Cover with plastic wrap. Microwave at High 5 minutes. Reduce power to 50% (Medium). Microwave 15 minutes.

Turn chicken over and rearrange so least cooked portions are to outside of dish. Microwave 20 to 30 minutes, or until chicken is fork tender and meat near bone is no longer pink.

Zippy Chicken ▲ & Vegetables

⅓ cup flour
1 envelope (0.6-oz.) old-fashioned French salad dressing mix
1 can (10¾-oz.) chicken broth
½ teaspoon bouquet sauce
4 medium carrots, thinly sliced (2 cups)
2 to 3 lbs. broiler-fryer chicken pieces
1 pkg. (10-oz.) frozen peas

Serves 4 to 6

Blend flour, salad dressing mix, broth and bouquet sauce in 3-qt. casserole until smooth. Add carrots and chicken. Cover with vented plastic wrap. Microwave at High 15 to 20 minutes, or until chicken loses almost all pink color. Stir in peas; rearrange chicken. Re-cover. Microwave 5 minutes. Stir and let stand, covered, 5 minutes before serving.

Cheddary Chicken, Rice ▶ & Tomatoes

1 can (16-oz.) whole tomatoes, chopped
1 can (11-oz.) cheddar cheese soup
2 cups quick-cooking rice
1 small onion, finely chopped
1 teaspoon basil
1 teaspoon salt
⅛ teaspoon pepper
2 to 3-lbs. broiler-fryer chicken pieces

Serves 4 to 6

In 12×8-in. dish combine tomatoes, soup, rice, onion and seasonings. Arrange chicken pieces on top, bony side up and meatiest portions to outside of dish. Cover with wax paper. Microwave at High 15 minutes.

Stir rice mixture and turn chicken pieces over. Microwave, uncovered, 11 to 15 minutes, or until chicken is fork tender and meat near bone is no longer pink.

How to Microwave Stuffed Chicken Thighs

Combine onion, celery, and butter in 2 cup measure. Microwave at High 1 to 2½ minutes, or until celery is tender. Stir in stuffing mix and water.

Lift skin on each thigh and put ¼ stuffing mix between meat and skin. Pull skin over stuffing. Arrange on roasting rack skin side up. If desired, brush with bouquet sauce mixture.

Microwave at High 8 minutes. Rearrange but do not turn thighs over. Microwave 7 to 10 minutes, or until chicken is fork tender and juices run clear.

Chicken Stir-Fry

Marinade:

¼ cup soy sauce
2 tablespoons vegetable oil
1 tablespoon dry sherry, optional

2 whole boneless chicken breasts, skinned and flattened
1 medium green pepper, cut in ¼ to ½-in. strips
½ cup sliced almonds
1 medium onion, thinly sliced, separated into rings

Serves 4

Combine marinade ingredients in small bowl. Set aside. Cut chicken into strips ¾ × 1½-in. Stir into marinade. Let stand at room temperature 15 to 30 minutes.

Preheat 10-in. browning dish at High 5 minutes. Quickly add chicken, marinade, green pepper and almonds. Stir briskly until sizzling slows. Mix in onions. Microwave at High 5½ to 8½ minutes, or until chicken strips are tender and no longer pink, stirring every 2 minutes. Serve over steamed rice with extra soy sauce, if desired.

How to Bone a Half Chicken Breast

Skin breast with your fingers. Sever the wing joint at the shoulder with a sharp knife. (Some breasts are sold without wings.)

Cut against breastbone to loosen meat. Angling sharp edge of knife toward bone, cut against ribs, pulling away meat as you cut.

Remove wing. Scrape and pull out tendon on under side of meat. Check with fingers for pieces of wishbone which may remain.

140

Chicken Breasts ▶ in Fruited Sour Cream Sauce

4 whole boneless chicken
   breasts, skinned
1 cup sour cream
½ cup apple juice
½ cup chopped dried apricots
2 tablespoons flour
1 teaspoon parsley flakes
¼ teaspoon salt

Serves 4

Place chicken in 8×8-in. dish. Cover with wax paper. Microwave at High 3 minutes.

While microwaving breasts, combine remaining ingredients in 1-qt. measure. Rearrange chicken and add sauce. Re-cover. Microwave 5 to 7 minutes, or until chicken is fork tender and no longer pink.

Artichoke-Stuffed Chicken Rolls

2 tablespoons butter or
   margarine
1½ tablespoons flour
1 teaspoon instant chicken
   bouillon
1 teaspoon chopped chives
½ teaspoon salt
⅛ teaspoon pepper
½ cup light cream
½ cup water

1 jar (6-oz.) marinated
   artichoke hearts, drained
   and chopped
½ cup shredded cheddar
   cheese
2 tablespoons seasoned
   bread crumbs
4 whole unsplit boneless
   chicken breasts, skinned
   and flattened to ¼-in.

Serves 4

In 1-qt. container, melt butter at High 30 to 50 seconds. Stir in flour, bouillon and seasonings until smooth. Blend in cream and water. Microwave at High 3 to 5 minutes, or until thickened, stirring twice during cooking. Set aside.

Combine artichoke hearts, cheese and bread crumbs in small bowl. Place ¼ of mixture in center of each chicken breast. Fold ends of chicken over stuffing and secure with wooden picks.

Place rolls seam side up in 8×8-in. dish. Cover with wax paper. Microwave at High 4 minutes. Drain.

Rearrange and turn rolls over. Pour sauce evenly over meat. Microwave, uncovered, 1½ to 3½ minutes, or until chicken is no longer pink.

How to Shape Chicken Rolls

Spread stuffing across center of unsplit boneless chicken breast. Fold ends over filling. Secure with wooden picks.

Chicken Coatings

Coatings give chicken flavor, variety and an attractive finish. To reduce calories, remove chicken skin and the fat beneath. The coatings will adhere to and flavor the meat directly. Each of these recipes will coat 2½ to 3 pounds of chicken pieces.

Fried Onion Coating

Coating:
2 cans (3-oz.) fried onion rings, crushed

Dip:
1 egg, beaten
2 tablespoons milk

Light Crumb Coating

Coating:
½ cup mashed potato flakes
½ cup seasoned bread crumbs
 1 teaspoon parsley flakes
½ teaspoon salt

Dip:
 5 tablespoons butter or
   margarine, melted

How to Microwave Coated Chicken Pieces

Combine coating ingredients in shallow dish or on wax paper. Set aside while preparing dip.

Dip chicken in mixture and dredge in coating. Press coarse coatings into place after dredging. Place pieces bone side down on rack with meatiest parts to outside. Microwave at High 10 minutes.

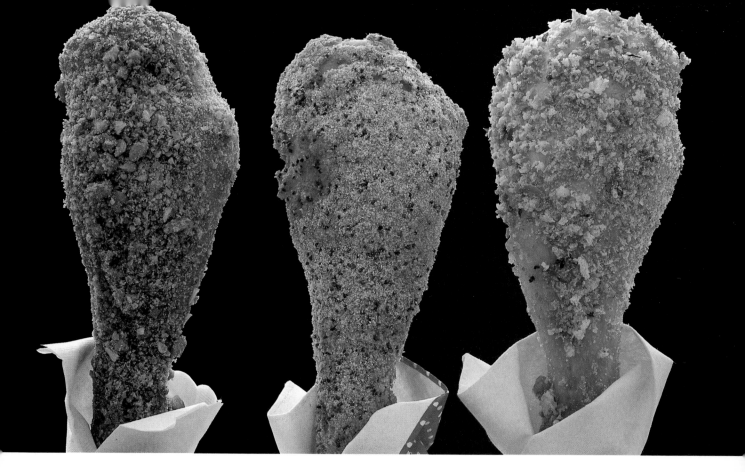

Savory Cracker Coating

Coating:
1½ cups (30 to 35) round buttery
 crackers, finely crushed
1 envelope (1-oz.) onion gravy
 mix

Dip:
1 egg, beaten
2 tablespoons milk

Corn Meal Coating

Coating:
¾ cup corn meal
2 tablespoons poppy seeds
2 teaspoons paprika

Dip:
2 eggs
4 tablespoons butter or
 margarine, melted

Herbed Coating

Coating:
1½ cups herb seasoned stuffing
 mix, finely crushed
¾ teaspoon basil leaves
⅛ to ¼ teaspoon garlic powder

Dip:
1 egg, beaten
2 tablespoons milk, or 1
 additional egg, beaten
4 tablespoons butter or
 margarine, melted

Rearrange so less cooked parts
are to outside of dish, but do not
turn chicken over.

Microwave at High 8 to 15 minutes, or until juices run clear and meat
near bone is no longer pink.

Open Faced Turkey-Bacon Sandwiches ▲

8 slices bacon
4 slices bread
1 package (1¼-oz.) cheese
   sauce mix

1 cup milk
8 slices cooked turkey
1 cup shredded Cheddar
   cheese

Serves 4

Microwave bacon as directed on page 94. Cut in half; set aside. Toast bread conventionally. Halve each slice and arrange in 12×8-in. dish. Combine cheese sauce mix and milk in 1-qt. casserole. Microwave at High 3 to 4 minutes, or until slightly thickened, stirring well after half the cooking time.

Place 2 bacon pieces on each toast half. Top with 1 turkey slice. Pour cheese sauce evenly over sandwiches. Sprinkle with shredded cheese. Cover with wax paper. Reduce power to 50% (Medium). Microwave 4½ to 6½ minutes, or until heated through, rotating dish after half the cooking time.

Poultry Leftovers

Any of these tasty main dishes can be microwaved quickly with either cooked turkey or chicken.

Turkey Tetrazzini

  2 cups sliced fresh
     mushrooms
  ¼ cup chopped onion
  ¼ cup butter or margarine
  ¼ cup flour
  ½ teaspoon salt
  ⅛ teaspoon nutmeg
  1 tablespoon instant chicken
     bouillon
  2 cups hot water
  ½ cup half & half
2½ cups cubed cooked turkey
  1 package (7-oz.) spaghetti,
     cooked
  ¼ cup Parmesan cheese
  ¼ cup seasoned bread
     crumbs
  ½ teaspoon paprika

Serves 4 to 6

Combine mushrooms and onion in 2-qt. casserole. Microwave at High 3 to 4 minutes, or until onion is translucent, stirring after half the cooking time. Remove vegetables from casserole and drain on paper towels.

Melt butter in casserole at High 45 to 60 seconds. Stir in flour, salt, and nutmeg until smooth. Microwave 30 to 40 seconds, or until bubbly. Dissolve bouillon in hot water; slowly stir into flour mixture. Microwave 4 to 6 minutes, or until thickened, stirring twice during cooking. Blend in half & half. Add mushrooms, onion and turkey.

Place spaghetti in 12×8-in. dish. Pour sauce mixture over spaghetti. Combine Parmesan cheese, bread crumbs and paprika in small mixing bowl. Sprinkle over casserole. Microwave at High 8 to 10 minutes, or until heated through, rotating dish after half the cooking time.

Chicken Enchiladas ▲

6 corn tortillas (If frozen,
   defrost by placing between
   paper towels and microwaving at High 45 to 60
   seconds.)

Filling:
2 cups cubed cooked chicken
8 oz. ricotta or cottage cheese
½ cup chopped ripe olives
2 teaspoons parsley flakes
½ teaspoon salt
⅛ teaspoon pepper
⅛ teaspoon garlic powder

Sauce:
1 medium onion, chopped
½ medium green pepper,
   chopped
1 can (15-oz.) tomato sauce
½ can (14-oz.) green chilies,
   drained and chopped,
   optional
2 teaspoons chili powder
1 teaspoon sugar
⅛ teaspoon garlic powder

Topping:
1½ cups shredded Cheddar
   cheese

Serves 4 to 6

Combine filling ingredients in medium mixing bowl. Divide evenly
into 6 portions. Place 1 portion of filling down center of each tortilla.
Roll up. Arrange seam side down in 12×8-in. dish.

Combine onion and green pepper in 1½-qt. casserole. Cover.
Microwave at High 3 to 4 minutes, or until vegetables are tender. Stir
in remaining sauce ingredients. Pour over filled tortillas. Cover with
wax paper. Microwave at High 7 to 10 minutes, or until heated
through. Sprinkle with Cheddar cheese.

Reduce power to 50% (Medium). Microwave uncovered 3 to 5
minutes, or until cheese melts.

Chicken A' la King

¼ cup butter or margarine
3 tablespoons flour
1 can (10¾-oz.) chicken broth
   Milk
2 cups cubed cooked chicken
   (or turkey)
½ teaspoon salt
¼ teaspoon pepper
1 cup cooked or canned peas
1 can (4-oz.) mushroom stems
   and pieces, drained
   Toast points

Serves 4

In 2-qt. casserole, melt butter at
High 45 to 60 seconds. Stir in
flour until smooth.

In 2-cup measure, combine
broth and enough milk to make 2
cups. Blend into flour mixture.
Microwave at High 5½ to 7½
minutes, or until thickened, stirring once or twice during cooking. Blend well.

Mix in remaining ingredients.
Microwave 2½ to 3½ minutes, or
until heated through. Serve over
toast points.

Turkey Stuffed Zucchini

2 medium zucchini, 7 to 8-in. long
1 teaspoon salt, divided
1 lb. boneless turkey, cut into
    ¼ × 1-in. strips
½ cup chopped onion
1 can (8¼-oz.) crushed
    pineapple, drained

¼ cup seasoned bread crumbs
1 teaspoon soy sauce
⅛ teaspoon pepper
¼ cup sliced almonds

Serves 4

Halve zucchini length-wise. Scoop out leaving ¼-in. shell, and chop pulp coarsely. Sprinkle zucchini shells with ¼ teaspoon salt. Set aside, cut side down, to drain.

Combine zucchini, turkey and onion in 2-qt. casserole. Cover. Microwave at High 5 to 7 minutes, or until turkey is no longer pink, stirring once after half the cooking time. Drain.

Stir in pineapple, bread crumbs, soy sauce, remaining ¾ teaspoon salt and pepper. Mound ¼ of the turkey mixture in each half zucchini shell.

Arrange stuffed zucchini in 8×8-in. dish. Cover with plastic wrap. Microwave 5 to 7 minutes, or until zucchini shells are tender.

Sprinkle almonds evenly over stuffing. Microwave, uncovered, 1 to 2 minutes, or until heated through.

Chicken Fried Rice

2 tablespoons butter or
    margarine
1 package (6¼-oz.) fried rice
    mix
2 cups cubed cooked chicken
1½ cups hot water
¼ cup chopped green pepper
¼ cup chopped green onion
¼ cup chopped carrots

Serves 4 to 6

Preheat 10-in. browning dish at High 5 minutes. Add butter and swirl to coat bottom of dish. Add rice from mix. (Butter or margarine need not be melted before adding rice.) Microwave at High 30 to 45 seconds, or until golden brown, stirring once during cooking. Stir in seasoning mix and remaining ingredients. Cover. Microwave 5 minutes. Reduce power to 50% (Medium). Microwave 14 to 19 minutes, or until rice is tender and water is absorbed.

Chicken & Vegetable Casserole

Sauce:
- 1 can (10¾-oz.) cream of chicken soup
- ½ cup mayonnaise or salad dressing
- 1 can (4-oz.) water chestnuts, chopped, optional
- 1½ teaspoons lemon juice
- ½ teaspoon prepared mustard
- ¼ teaspoon curry powder

- 1 package (10-oz.) frozen mixed vegetables
- 2 cups, ½-in. cubes, cooked chicken or turkey
- ⅔ cup shredded cheddar cheese
- ¼ cup seasoned bread crumbs

Serves 4 to 6

Combine sauce ingredients well. Microwave frozen vegetables in box at High 3 to 4 minutes, or until defrosted. Drain.

In 1½-qt. casserole, layer half the vegetables, half the chicken, half the sauce, and half the cheese. Repeat. Top with bread crumbs.

Microwave at High 3 minutes. Reduce power to 50% (Medium). Microwave 10 to 12 minutes, or until heated through, rotating dish after half the cooking time.

Chicken & Wild Rice

- ½ cup chopped celery
- ½ cup chopped onion
- ¼ cup wild rice
- 2 tablespoons butter or margarine
- 1 can (10¾-oz.) chicken broth
- 1 cup water
- ½ teaspoon salt
- ¼ teaspoon rosemary
- ⅛ teaspoon sage
- 1½ cups cubed cooked chicken
- 1 can (4-oz.) mushroom stems and pieces, drained
- ½ cup long grain rice

Serves 4

In 2-qt. casserole, combine celery, onion, rice and butter. Cover. Microwave at High 3 to 4 minutes, or until vegetables are tender. Stir in chicken broth, water and seasonings. Cover tightly. Microwave at High 5 minutes. Reduce power to 50% (Medium). Microwave 30 minutes. Stir in chicken, mushrooms and rice. Cover. Microwave 25 to 30 minutes, or until rice is tender.

Duck

Duckling renders a lot of fat, so the skin browns naturally. Fat should be drained several times during cooking because it draws microwave energy and can make the dish difficult to handle.

Start at High
First 10 min.

Finish at 50% (Medium)
7-9 min. per lb.

How to Microwave Duckling

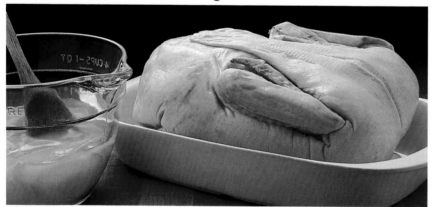

Prepare glaze or sauce. Remove giblets and wash duckling. Place on rack, breast side down. Estimate the total cooking time; divide in half. Microwave at High first 10 minutes. Drain well.

Secure neck skin to back with wooden picks. Fill cavity with flavoring ingredients.

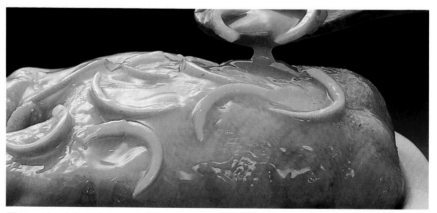

Return duckling to rack, breast side down. Reduce power to 50% (Medium). Microwave remaining part of first half of time. Drain fat from dish.

Turn duckling breast side up. Glaze or spoon sauce over breast as directed in recipe. Microwave remaining time. Drain fat. Add more glaze or sauce. Let stand, tented with foil, shiny side in, 5 minutes.

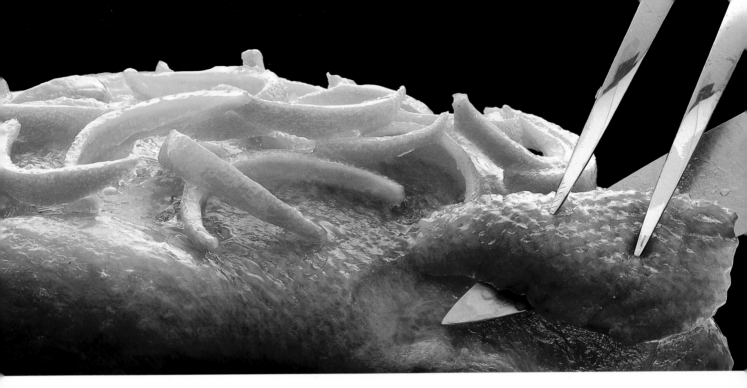

Duck A L'Orange ▲

4½ to 5½-lb. duckling

Glaze:
    1 orange
    2 tablespoons cornstarch
    2 tablespoons sugar
    1 cup orange juice
    ¼ cup sherry
    2 tablespoons vinegar

Cavity:
    1 medium onion, cut in eighths
    Reserved orange from glaze

Peel orange, being careful not to remove the white membrane. Cut peel into julienne strips; place in 1-qt. container. Cut orange into fourths and reserve fruit for stuffing duck.

Mix cornstarch and sugar into container with orange peel. Stir in remaining glaze ingredients. Microwave at High 4 to 5 minutes, or until thickened, stirring twice during cooking. Set aside.

Prepare and microwave duckling, following photo directions. Spoon on ⅓ of sauce during microwaving, ⅓ before standing time and serve remaining sauce with duck.

Peachy Duck

4½ to 5½-lb. duckling

Glaze:
    1 can (16-oz.) sliced peaches, reserve ½ cup juice
    2 teaspoons cornstarch
    2 tablespoons lemon juice
    1 tablespoon brown sugar
    ½ teaspoon prepared mustard
    ¼ teaspoon salt
    ⅛ teaspoon curry powder

Cavity:
    1 medium onion, cut in eighths
    1 stalk celery, quartered

Combine peach juice and cornstarch in 1-qt. measure. Blend in remaining glaze ingredients except peaches. Microwave at High 2½ to 4½ minutes, or until thickened. Stir with fork until smooth.

Coarsely chop peaches and stir into glaze. Set aside.

Prepare and microwave duckling, following photo directions. Use half the glaze during microwaving and remainder before standing time.

Plum Duck

4½ to 5½-lb. duckling

Glaze:
    8 oz. fresh mushrooms, sliced
    1 jar (12-oz.) plum preserves
    ½ teaspoon allspice

Cavity:
    2 stalks celery, cut in 2-in. pieces

Place mushrooms in 1-qt. casserole. Cover. Microwave at High 3 to 5 minutes, or until mushrooms are tender, stirring after half the cooking time. Drain. Stir in preserves and allspice. Set aside.

Prepare and microwave duckling, following photo directions. Use half the glaze during microwaving and remainder before standing time.

Apple-Maple Variation:
Omit glaze ingredients. In small bowl, combine ½ cup chunky applesauce, ¼ cup maple-flavored syrup, ¼ teaspoon ground cinnamon, ¼ teaspoon ground cloves. Stuff and cook duck as directed above, using applesauce mixture as glaze.

Cornish Hens

Tender cornish hens microwave quickly at High power. Due to their small size, low fat content and short cooking time, they will not brown. Diluted bouquet sauce, soy sauce or a glaze gives them an attractive finish.

High Power
5½-8 min. per lb.

How to Microwave Cornish Hens

Place breast side down in baking dish. Brush with equal parts bouquet sauce and butter or water. Cover with wax paper. Microwave at High for ¼ the time.

Rotate dish ½ turn. Microwave for ¼ of time. Turn breast side up, so sides which were near edge of dish are in center.

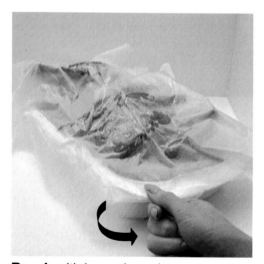

Brush with browning mixture. Microwave ¼ of time. Rotate dish ½ turn.

◄ Stuffed Game Hens

Stuffing:
¼ cup chopped onion
¼ cup butter or margarine
2 cups herb seasoned stuffing
  mix
⅔ cup hot water
1 can (8¼-oz.) crushed
  pineapple, well drained

¼ to ½ teaspoon poultry
  seasoning
4 cornish hens
1 tablespoon butter or
  margarine
1 tablespoon bouquet sauce

Serves 4

In 1-qt. measure, microwave onion and butter at High 2 to 3½ minutes, or until onion is translucent. Blend in remaining stuffing ingredients. Stuff each hen with ¼ the stuffing mixture, secure cavity opening with wooden picks, if desired. Place hens breast side down on roasting rack. Set aside.

In 1 cup measure, microwave remaining butter 20 to 45 seconds, or until melted. Blend in bouquet sauce. Lightly brush hens with half the mixture. Cover with wax paper. Microwave 15 minutes, rotating dish ½ turn after 7 minutes.

Turn hens breast side up. Brush with remaining bouquet sauce mixture. Cover with wax paper. Microwave 16 to 19 minutes, or until legs move freely and juices run clear, rotating dish ½ turn after 8 minutes.

Game Hens Stuffed With Rice

1 package (6¼-oz.) quick
  cooking long grain and
  wild rice mix
¼ cup chopped onion
⅓ cup coarsely chopped
  cashews

4 cornish hens
1 tablespoon butter or
  margarine
1 tablespoon bouquet sauce

Serves 4

In 1½-qt. casserole, combine rice, seasoning packet, water and butter as package directs. Cover tightly. Microwave at High 5 minutes. Reduce power to 50% (Medium). Microwave 4 to 6 minutes, or until rice is tender and water is absorbed. Stir in onion and nuts. Stuff each hen with ¼ the rice mixture and secure opening with wooden picks, if desired. Place hens breast side down on roasting rack.

In custard cup, melt butter at High 20 to 45 seconds. Blend in bouquet sauce. Brush each hen with butter mixture. Cover with wax paper. Microwave at High 15 minutes; rotate dish after half the time.

Rearrange hens and turn breast side up. Brush with butter mixture. Re-cover. Microwave 16 to 19 minutes, or until legs move freely and juices run clear; rotate dish after half the time. Reheat any extra stuffing by microwaving at High ½ to 1¼ minutes; use as garnish.

NOTE: When microwaving 2 cornish hens reduce cooking times to 10 minutes and 8 to 10 minutes.

Microwave remaining time, or until leg moves easily and juices run clear. Let stand covered, 5 to 10 minutes.

Index

152